Left For Dead

by

Rose Frost

PublishAmerica
Baltimore

ISBN: 1-4137-8900-5
PUBLISHED BY PUBLISHAMERICA, LLLP
www.publishamerica.com
Baltimore

Printed in the United States of America

Chapter One

The dirt road was long and lonely as it wound its way through the hills. Being the middle of May the trees were bright with their new spring growth – the oaks and the dogwoods, the pines and the redbuds all giving the forest a look that, while incredibly beautiful in every direction, isolated every curve of the road from those before and after it, adding dramatically to the lonely feelings one experienced driving over that road.

With the blossoming of spring in all it's vibrant colors, the brush filling out to cover the hills in a lush coat of green, the extraordinary beauty of the bluffs were often hidden from view and would not be seen again until autumn cleared the view with the falling of the leaves. But the bluffs were there – tall, majestic, towering over their kingdom below.

One lone car wound its way through the lonely hills on that early Sunday evening. For more than forty minutes it had not passed another vehicle, and it was not likely to do so again for another half hour or more. Being national forest land there hadn't even been any occupied homes for miles – adding dramatically to the isolation of the road.

Only one person was out there in those woods – one man as lonely as the road, toting a squirrel gun, hunting his dinner. At first he paid no attention to the sound of the approaching car, intent as he was on his pursuit, as unaccustomed as he was to any traffic being found so far from the main highway. But as the sound grew nearer in the otherwise still air of the growing dusk, instinct made him suddenly alert.

No one driving by was likely to see him so far below the surface of the road, hidden as he was in the shadows of the evening, even should they bother to look. The bluffs between him and the road were at least three hundred feet high. Even if someone should spot him here it was unlikely they should give him a second thought. But caution was instinctive, and fear gripped him as the car pulled to a stop at the top of the bluff overhead, the engine stilled to silence.

Why had they stopped? his frantic mind wondered. Why would anyone stop here, in this particular spot, now – in the growing darkness of evening? Were they only tourists wishing for one last look at the view? He hoped so. Yet he held no faith in that hope as the sun had already gone down and nighttime darkness was not far off. What could they see of the view at this time of day?

Yet could they possibly be here about him? No one knew he was here. For more than a year now he had been completely safe from detection in this isolated section of forest. Surely there was no reason to believe that had changed.

Even so, he was prepared to make his escape should the slightest hint of danger be presented. And he would escape. Unless the person intended to just drop straight over the bluff it would take at least ten minutes for anyone to reach the river bank. He knew the area. They would not find him. And yet he was alert as he had not been in a year.

Being across the river from the bluff, even so far below the road, he was able to see the car – a red sports car, possibly a Ferrari, though in the growing darkness he could not be certain from this distance. Two people got out of the car, both dressed in jeans, but even from this distance he could see they were both female and an acute sense of relief swept through him. They would never have sent women after him. Despite the growing darkness they were here only for the view.

Even so, even knowing that their interest could not be in him personally, as they walked to the edge of the bluff to look at the valley below, he was careful to keep himself hidden from their view behind the trees, continually watchful of their every move.

They were talking peacefully about the view. From this distance he could hear none of their words, but the quiet hum of their voices as it floated down to him was calm and good-natured, their movements friendly and relaxed as one woman, the taller of the two, standing slightly behind the shorter, pointed out different sights in the distance for the other's attention.

They were just tourists, he thought, feeling his heart relax. They would look at the view for a moment, get back into their car, and leave his world without any awareness of him at all. He was still safe here in these godforsaken, lonely hills, all alone…

Suddenly – in an amazingly swift act – the taller woman lifted something in her hand behind the smaller woman, bringing it crashing down on her head with such force that her victim collapsed to the ground in an instant. No longer was the smaller woman visible to the man below as the taller woman knelt over her lifeless form, but there was no doubt as to her condition. If she was not dead already from that blow she soon would be.

Shock at the sight he had just witnessed brought the terrors of his past back to the man's mind so vividly he couldn't move. Flashes of memory that refused to die completely, even after two years time, now filled him as he watched, not the murder of an unknown woman on the road above, but Diane falling into death at his feet so long ago.

With a shudder he forced the memory from his mind. To let such thoughts have their way would serve only to drive him completely out of his mind. This was not Diane. This was a complete stranger. He could stay detached. He would. He had to for the sake of his own sanity.

Watching, he saw the taller of the two women still kneeling over her victim, though he was unable to see just what she was doing, and for a moment he entertained the idea that maybe he should do something – for his own protection. Would this woman's dead body be left out here with him? If so, and if it should be spotted by the next tourist who stopped to admire the view, would it bring the authorities looking for evidence?

He knew it would, and he knew what they would do to him. With his record, his conviction, his status as a fugitive from justice, he would be sent back to prison instantly. They may even accuse him of this woman's death as well, and he would never be free again.

Should he get a closer look at the woman and her car – get a license number just in case he had to defend himself later? But he knew the futility of such an attempt. Unless he could sprout wings and fly to the top of that bluff there was no way he could reach the top in time. A woman in her position was not going to wait around the scene of her crime long enough to be identified by the likes of him.

She moved again. Taking her victim by the hands, she dragged her lifeless form to the very edge of the bluff, moved to her side, and calmly rolled her over the edge.

Feelings of nausea filled him as he watched the now naked form of the woman fall through the air. He understood the reasons for removing her clothing. It would be ages – months, even years maybe – before her body would be discovered down there at the bottom of the bluff. By then her features would be unrecognizable. If neither her fingerprints nor DNA were on file anywhere they may never be able to identify her even should she be found.

The tall woman watched her fall, watched as the naked, lifeless form of her companion fell into the brush below – brush that would in no time at all have grown up to cover her completely. She then walked out of his view for a moment, returning with a branch with which she erased all trace of her having dragged a body to the edge of the cliff. That finished, she tossed the branch after her companion, picked up the clothing she'd removed from her victim, and a moment later was roaring away in her car.

Shock and horror at all he'd witnessed kept the man where he was for a long moment as he fought to keep the picture of Diane's lifeless body lying in a pool of blood at his feet from overtaking him completely. Whatever anyone might say, such pictures did not go away. They would haunt him as long as he lived. Nor would he ever cease to regret that day until he finally saw that same fate himself.

But this was not Diane, he reminded himself again. This was a total stranger. He could stay detached in this case, like watching a movie. He could forget what he'd seen as quickly as forgetting the scene of a movie on a screen.

Yet could he? It was not just the haunting of his past that involved him, it was his future. If anyone spotted this woman's body– If they came snooping around looking for clues– If they blamed him–

What if he buried her? If she was out of sight, if no one ever saw her, there was no reason for anyone to come snooping around. And if no one came snooping around then no one would find him. He would be safe.

Having landed in the brush at the base of the bluff, the body was now out of his sight, but he knew where it had landed, and it was just possible that, looking down from the road above, a person could see it where it lay. He should at least investigate, analyze any danger to himself its presence might cause.

Slinging the squirrel gun over his shoulder, his personal quest for dinner forgotten, he made his way upstream about fifty feet to a point where he could cross without getting too wet. It was then only a matter of a couple minutes before he reached the spot where he'd seen the body land, but it took another couple minutes to get through the brush to reach her side.

Having broken her fall at least to some extent, the brush was still holding her captive. The delicate skin of her young body was torn and scraped badly by the same brush, as well as by the rock she'd bumped against often on her way down, and the blood from her wounds at first made him too nauseous to think.

But he forced himself past that, forced himself to stay detached as he had once before so long ago. The important thing right now was to get her body out of sight so that no one connected her to him.

Something about her touched him as he lifted her from the brush that held her. She was so tiny, so delicate – a hundred pounds, a hundred ten at most, he judged – and, despite her wounds, incredibly beautiful. Her hair – a long, dark silk – covered her naked breasts as he found her, but quickly fell away as he lifted her in his arms and carried her to the flat ground along the river bank where he laid her, kneeling beside her.

Some unknown compulsion caused him to feel for her pulse even when he saw little hope of finding one after all that had just happened to her. Maybe it was just that she was too beautiful to be dead. Maybe it was the memories of Diane lying at his feet that prompted him to be absolutely certain of her condition before he acted.

To his astonishment he felt a thready, very weak pulse at her throat. She was alive. As incredible as it was, the blow to her head and the subsequent fall had not killed her. Apparently the brush, while cutting her delicate skin terribly, had softened her fall enough to prevent her from being killed outright.

It was likely only temporary, though. It would probably only be minutes before she was dead, even with his help, and yet he bent his face next to hers to check for breathing. As shallow, as barely discernible as it was, he could feel her breath on his skin.

So what next? Bleeding. She had several open wounds, but only two he felt worthy of immediate concern – one on her head where the original blow had been struck, and one on her left leg which he felt certain was broken. He had no bandage material out here, so he ripped a couple strips from his shirt tail, then applied pressure to the wounds until he felt they had stopped bleeding sufficiently.

Shock. Wasn't that the next thing to consider? He had no real first-aid training, but he felt certain after injuries as serious as these shock would most likely be a great danger. Keep her warm, he thought. With the setting of the sun the air had been cooling for some time, and in the continuously lowered temperature, without even the benefit of clothing, she was in serious danger of being chilled with or without the danger of shock.

Not even thinking, he gave her the only warmth to which he had access, his shirt. There was no need to bother putting her arms through the sleeves in her state of unconsciousness, so he just wrapped the shirt around her body and buttoned it up over her to provide as much warmth as possible.

Now he turned his attention to her leg. Should he splint it here before moving her? Probably, he thought. But he really had nothing here to use. There were plenty of sticks to use as splints, but unless he intended ripping off more of his shirt he had nothing to use to hold the splints in place. And wasn't it more important to keep her warm just now?

He didn't know. Without first-aid training he was far from expert on the subject. But he did have experience with broken bones, and surely it wouldn't hurt her any more than she already was to wait until they reached the cabin to worry about this break.

Gently, with great care not to add to her injuries, he lifted her into his arms again, holding her so that her head rested on his shoulder rather than hanging limply over his arm, and carried her back across the river.

It would take twenty minutes, maybe more with this weight in his arms, light as she was, to reach the cabin. Would that be too late? Would the cool temperatures be too much for her? Would shock take over? Even if he got her to the cabin alive there was no guarantee she would stay that way. He was not a doctor. He had no way of knowing the extent of any internal injuries she might have. Nor could he deal with them if he did.

Knowing nothing else to do, he just held her as close as possible as he walked, hoping his body heat would be enough to keep her alive.

Why he cared what happened to this woman he didn't know. She was a stranger. Maybe like Diane she deserved the hatred that had led her companion to plot the taking of her life this way. Maybe her violent death was only an act of justice.

He did not help her for her benefit. He did not make such efforts on her behalf because she was beautiful and deserving. In fact, should she survive – despite the odds – it meant he would have revealed himself to a stranger, he would have put his own freedom, maybe even his life, into danger for a woman he didn't even know and really could not care less about.

The danger to himself was real, and yet, for the sake of his own sanity, he could not leave her to die without at least trying to save her. Maybe in some small way he could make up for that horrible day so long ago. Maybe his efforts to save this woman could give his tormented conscience a measure of relief for past mistakes, and ease the nightmares that thus far had refused to give him any peace.

The fire in the rusty old stove was still going when finally he reached the cabin with his load. Though she still had a pulse and was still breathing as he laid her on his bed, both were so weak as to be barely discernible, and he feared it would be only a matter of time before they faded away to nothing.

With apparently nothing he could do to prevent that from happening, though, he could only keep her warm and watch for trouble, so he wrapped the blankets around her, and sat on one of the two chairs at the table to watch her.

What had she done to merit such anger that had led another human being to attempt her murder and leave her for dead? he wondered as he stared at her. Had she betrayed a trust as Diane had? Had she cheated on her husband? Was she pregnant with another man's child – the child of a man she had seduced with delight? Had she laughed at her deceit, at the betrayal of her vows?

Yet it was a woman who had struck that blow and rolled her off the bluff, not a jealous husband or a jealous lover. Could she have been the lover's wife out for revenge? Yet their ride had been friendly. As they'd viewed together the valley below there had been a trust between them or this woman would never have allowed herself to be caught by surprise that way.

Nor had it been an angry outburst which had prompted that act. It had been clearly premeditated. The drive had been planned, the site carefully chosen, the weapon kept handy to be used when the time was right. Even the removal of her clothing showed careful thought in not wanting the body to be identified should it be found.

So what was behind this? And how deeply was he going to be involved? Would someone come looking for her here when it was found she was missing? It seemed unlikely. This place had clearly been chosen to avoid having her found, at least not any time soon. At least for now he should be free from detection.

But how would this woman react to him if and when she recovered enough to face him? Would she be grateful enough to him for rescuing her to keep his secret? Or would she recognize him from the many, many times his face had been in the media? Would she be terrified of him? Would she feel it her duty to turn him in to the authorities despite his caring for her?

Maybe it would be safer for him if he took her someplace else before she awoke. He could carry her to some house down the road while she was still unconscious, where she could get to a hospital and help without seeing him or knowing of his involvement.

And yet he dismissed that thought for several reasons – almost as soon as it occurred to him. For one, the nearest house of which he was aware was at least ten miles away – taking the shortest route. To reach it carrying an unconscious body would take all day. There was no telling what her condition would be like after a trip like that.

Nor could he be sure anyone would be there when he arrived. He knew many of the houses in the forest had been empty for years, even decades, and most of the ones that were still used were seasonal dwellings at best. He could carry her all that way only to find no help available for her at all.

Even if he did find her some help somewhere without being spotted, if and when she came to she was bound to remember what had happened to her, and curiosity about how she had managed to get from the sight of her attack to the sight of her rescue would certainly bring her back looking for answers. He would not have helped himself in any way.

And what about his shirt? Unless he abandoned her to the unknown help as naked as he'd found her, the shirt she now wore would lead her back to him. There would be nothing left for him to do but to pack up his life, such as it was, and move on, hoping against hope that no one followed his trail.

His freedom likely depended on him doing that anyway, but he would cross that bridge when he came to it. Until then he would just have to look after her the best way he could, and hope his humanitarian act would be taken into consideration later.

She looked so pale lying there on his bed and, as he watched her still and silent form, Diane's face took her place despite the fact they were so very different. While Diane had been a natural fiery redhead, this woman had long, silky black hair. While Diane had been tall and curvaceous – with long, shapely legs and a bust that wouldn't quit – this woman was petite from head to toe.

But it wasn't her figure or her beauty that he was seeing now. It was the blood on her head, blood that flooded his mind and body with the remembered nausea he'd felt at the sight of Diane lying at his feet so long ago.

It was blood that did it. Every time he caught sight of blood since that day the nausea returned. If he killed a squirrel or a rabbit for his dinner he felt it. If he pricked his finger on a thorn the sight even of his own blood brought the nausea flooding back. He couldn't escape it, nor could he dismiss the guilt that came with it.

But this was not Diane. This was not the terror of that fateful day. This was a nameless woman he had never seen before. If he could only keep reminding himself of that fact he could keep himself detached and objective.

Getting to his feet, he went to her side, kneeling beside the bed to feel again for her pulse. Maybe if he bathed her wounds and bound her leg in some sort of splint, if he had something constructive to concentrate on, if he removed the sight of her blood from his vision — maybe he could get Diane out of his mind.

The big steel kettle was in its accustomed place on the wood stove, and the water in it was steaming hot. With his ladle he dipped some of the water into his only bowl, added a ladle full of cold water from the bucket on the table to adjust the temperature, and, using the cleanest rag he could find, concentrated on bathing the large wound on her head where her companion had struck, apparently with considerable malice.

Having bathed her most serious wound, as well as the smaller ones on her face and neck where the brush had cut her skin, he made an amateurish bandage out of more clean rags, then turned his attention to her leg.

So as not to let her body cool off any more than necessary, he left the blankets over her as much as possible, uncovering only as much of her left leg as necessary to set her shin bone. The wound on the outside of her shin had dirt and rock bits embedded in the flesh as if she had slammed it into a protruding chunk of the bluff face on her way down. The fracture could be felt on the inner part of her leg across from the wound. The bone had not penetrated the skin, but he could feel it poking into her flesh from underneath.

Broken bones were one thing he did know about from personal experience. As a child he had broken an arm during a rather involved game of tackle football with his friends, and he knew the importance of setting the bone as soon as possible, not just to ensure proper healing, but to prevent further damage to the flesh around it.

First, though, he bathed the wound, carefully ignoring the nausea that would not go away at the sight of the grossly marred flesh stained with blood and dirt. Once he had it as clean as he could reasonably get it, he wrapped more rags around it as a bandage. He then went in search of splinting material before attempting to set the bone.

It was a good thing she was already unconscious, he thought as he pulled the leg slowly and carefully toward him until he felt the bone slip back in place. Otherwise the pain would have knocked her out. Remembering his own pain at the broken bone of his youth helped keep him focused on the task at hand.

Once finished with her major wounds he contemplated dealing with her minor ones. He knew her body was covered with cuts and bruises that should probably be cleaned to prevent infection. Yet he was loath to touch her naked body to bathe them. Diane's taunting, haunting words filled his mind, her mocking laughter tearing at his soul. He could not forget the anger and humiliation he had felt – the feelings with which her verbal abuse had filled him that day would plague him forever.

"Do you think I actually enjoyed the touch of your miserable hands on my flesh?" she had jeered. "I despised it. My skin crawls even now at just the thought of you touching me."

Shock had filled him at her words. He had not believed her. How could such words be true? Had he not felt the eagerness of her response to his touch only the night before? And yet, when he reminded her of their shared passion, she had shown him a side to her personality he had never seen before. In an instant the taunting, hateful look on her face had changed to the innocent, loving, devoted woman he had married, who had shared his bed only the night before.

"Darling," she had said then with feeling while wrapping her arms around his neck, kissing him with all the fire he had known she possessed.

And then she had pushed him away, her derisive laughter chilling him through. "Darling," she'd said again, mocking him with a cruelty he had not known she possessed. "Look at those hands, those rough, dirty, calloused hands. Do you think I could enjoy those hands mauling me when I can have the sensitive touch of Steve's perfect hands? Do not kid yourself, My Dear. Now that I carry Steve's child he wants me with him. I shall never have to endure your touch again. You may save them for the dogs they are more suited to, because no woman is going to want you touching her again."

He had not responded well to her evil taunting. Her words had been more than a betrayal of his trust and his love. They had shaken the very foundation of his self-confidence. Not only was she pregnant with another man's child, a man he had trusted in his own employ, but she had found him laughingly inadequate and distasteful personally. She had abhorred his very touch.

Looking down now at his hands he knew the truth of her words. If anything the hard work he'd put them through out here in the wilds of the forest had made them even rougher and more calloused than when she had mocked them. If the woman who had vowed to love him forever abhorred his touch, this stranger would even more so not want him touching the more sensitive parts of her flesh.

Quickly he drew the blanket back over her leg and stood up. Just knowing who he was would disgust and terrify her. If she thought he had mauled her unconscious body while she was unable to defend herself or even express her distaste, she would be outraged. Still, if she awoke to find herself bound inside his shirt as she was, unable to move her arms freely, wouldn't that terrify her even more?

He couldn't take that chance. Pulling the blankets back down off her body, he quickly set about the task of slipping her arms through the sleeves. At least that would leave her free to defend herself upon awakening – if she awoke. He then covered her back up. He could do nothing more for her. It was up to her body's own defenses now.

Taking his squirrel gun with him, he went into the night. It was dark now, but the moon was at three quarters, so he was able to see where he was going without difficulty. Even so, his hunt for some meat for his dinner was fruitless, and finally he returned to the cabin empty handed to find his guest in the same condition as he'd left her. Her breathing and her pulse were still there, but still very weak. Only time would tell if she would improve, or if his efforts to save her had been in vain.

That night was a long one for the young man with the critically injured guest. Having neglected to procure any fresh meat for his dinner, he'd had to do with a dish of vegetables and a few slices of the rabbit jerky he had made himself. Provisions were getting low again – the vegetables in the cellar were getting old and the ones in his garden had yet to produce.

Having given his bed – uncomfortable as it might be – and his blankets to his guest, he had to make do on the hardwood floor with only a rug to give him any protection from it's cold surface, making sleep nearly impossible. A dozen times during the night his dreams tormented him into wakefulness, whereupon he would get up, stoke the fire, and check on his guest once again.

Sometime in the night the young woman developed a fever and his concern grew. A fever could not be a good sign. As he had no medical experience he couldn't be sure of the cause or what to do about it, but when her fever had her growing delirious he knew he had to do something.

All he knew to do was to bathe her feverish face with cold, wet rags and hope for the best. Later, when that seemed to be of no help, he placed small amounts of water in her mouth with his spoon, carefully holding her head up so the water would drip into her throat without chocking her.

For hours he alternated periods of restless sleep on the cold, hard floor, with attempts to relieve her distress with cold rags on her face and cold water on her tongue. Morning came, and still her fever persisted. But then, rather than trying to rest between his nursing stints, he began his day's chores.

There was wood to chop for the fire, food to procure for breakfast, water to carry from the spring for drinking, washing the few dishes and clothes he possessed. There was the garden to attend to, the traps to check and eggs to hunt. The other things – clearing the gathering debris from the spring, mending the hole in the outhouse roof and gathering the honey and beeswax from the hive he'd discovered – would have to wait, even though he had planned them for today.

Every half-hour or less, whatever task in which he was involved, he returned to his patient to bathe her feverish face and cool her tongue with drops of water. Every time he returned it was with the expectation that he would find his efforts had failed and he would be faced with the task of burying her lifeless body. But each time he was relieved to find her breathing and as feverish as before.

Finally, during the second night, her fever broke. As before he had done what he could for her regularly throughout the night between bouts of fitful sleep on the floor, and just as the sky was starting to grow light with the new day's sun he was back at her side to find the fever gone.

His first thought was that it was over, that the fever had taken its toll and now she was cooling off as death had claimed her. But then he became aware of her breathing, breathing that was stronger and more even than before. A sense of pride filled him to think maybe he had saved her life after all.

Even so, despite the fever having left her, she did not regain consciousness. As often as before he left his chores that second day to return to her side. No longer did he bathe her face as he had, but he did continue spooning water into her mouth to prevent dehydration. It was the only thing he knew to do for her now.

A number of things were scarce in the cabin. The dishes he possessed were sufficient to get him by, but feeding a guest was another story. Ammunition for the squirrel gun was used only when the traps were unproductive, and then only if reaching the target was a sure thing. And the candles he'd formed from beeswax last fall were used extremely sparingly.

Clothing was another item of which he had too little – his wardrobe consisting only of two pairs of blue jeans, four pairs of socks, three shirts, and two pairs of undershorts.

Daily he washed out the clothes he'd worn the day before and hung them to dry for the next day. That had been sufficient until now. But now he was forced to share his meager possessions with the woman who still slept in his bed. So far all she was using was one shirt, but that would not do for long once she was awake.

Extra blankets and an extra bed would also be nice, he thought as he took his place on the floor for the third night in a row. But he was beginning to get used to it, just as he'd gotten used to the lumpy mattress on that bed after countless sleepless nights had moved him past caring. He'd proven he could get used to anything. But how would his guest handle the primitive conditions? He dreaded finding out.

With sunrise he was up again as usual to do the chores and that morning he managed to catch two small trout for his breakfast. That, with the two pheasant eggs he'd found, constituted his meal and he was just removing them from the pan to his plate when a movement from the bed caught his attention. Turning, he saw his guest staring at him with blank eyes.

"Good morning," he said, his voice, unaccustomed as it was to speaking aloud, echoing eerily through the cabin.

Placing his plate on the table, he gave it one last regretful look as he contemplated the fact he would now have to share it.

"You want some breakfast?" he asked.

The dark eyes of the young woman followed his movement, but otherwise there was no response from her.

"Are you thirsty?" he suggested.

Still she gave no response, but her eyes followed him as he dipped some water into his only cup and brought it to her.

"It's fresh and cold," he said as he held it out to her. But she made no attempt to take it, just stared at him in silence.

She knows who I am, he thought. She knows and she's terrified.

"I'll just put it here in case you want it," he said, placing the cup on the wooded box that often served him as a chair, then backing away to put her at her ease. But she did not pick up the cup, though her eyes followed his every movement.

"If you're hungry there's trout and eggs," he said. "Nothing gourmet, but it's adequate for staving off starvation."

Still she said nothing. Did she prefer to starve rather than to trust him to feed her? But no, as he looked closer into her face, he realized it was not fear of him that he saw there, but rather it was the blank stare of eyes with no thought behind them whatsoever, the stare of a new born infant whose eyes followed the movement around him but understood nothing of what it meant.

Slowly he walked to the other side of the room and back again, watching her eyes as he went. They followed his every movement, but always with that same blank stare. He moved to the bed and knelt at her side, that blank stare following him.

"How do you feel?" he asked, but there was no answer.

He got to his feet again and returned to the table to eat his breakfast in thoughtful silence. Was he to be stuck with a brain-damaged invalid? Had he saved her from death only to confine her to an existence without conscious awareness of the world around her?

How could he deal with that? He could barely take care of himself. It wasn't even reasonable to contemplate taking care of her day after day in that condition. He had only one choice. He would have to carry her out of here, take back his shirt, remove the splint and the bandages, and hope that whoever found her thought she had just been wandering through the forest on her own so that he would not be connected with her at all.

As despicable as he found that option, he saw it as his only choice. Right after breakfast he would have to be on his way.

Chapter Two

As the young man turned from his breakfast he saw that his guest was again sleeping. He may as well take care of his chores before setting off to carry her out of his life. For a trip like that he would need food and water, even his sleeping bag would be a good idea in case it took him that long with carrying her – as he had no way of knowing just how far he would have to travel to find her adequate help.

As he made the rounds of his traps his thoughts were mixed. The last thing he needed was the responsibility of caring for a woman who couldn't care for herself. If she remained this incoherent it would mean feeding her and bathing her. It would mean permanently giving up his bed to her and changing his whole schedule to look after her as one would an infant. He couldn't do it. He wouldn't do it. It wasn't fair that he should even be faced with the decision to do so.

And yet he knew a curiosity that craved satisfaction. Who was she? Why had her companion viewed her with such hatred as to premeditate her murder and dispose of her body so carefully? And what was going to happen to her if and when she was returned to her world? Would a second attempt be made on her life?

That thought not having occurred to him before, he wrestled with it in his mind from one trap to the next. In her present condition she would be unable to defend herself or even to accuse her attacker. Would her companion take advantage of that fact to finish the job she had started? Or would she decide the woman was no threat as she was now and leave her alone?

But this woman was not his responsibility. It wasn't his concern what happened to her in the future. He'd saved her life, at least for now. All he could do was return her to her world. If that world could not protect her it was certainly not his problem. Besides, did it really matter what happened to her body if her mind was so completely unaware of it?

By the time he'd returned to the cabin he was convinced that taking her out of there was the right thing to do. He would prepare the two rabbits he'd just found in the traps as food for the trip and be on his way. The sooner he disposed of his unwanted house guest the better.

To his surprise he opened the door to find his guest sitting up in bed, the cup of water he'd left near her now half-empty in her hand.

"Thank you," she said in a voice as sweet as honey as she lifted the cup in acknowledgment before swallowing the last of the water with a thirsty eagerness.

"You're welcome," he said. His words, unaccustomed as he was to speaking aloud, came out as a whisper of surprise while he stared at her. Maybe she wasn't as bad off as he'd feared. Maybe she had just been groggy before. Given time, maybe she would be perfectly alright.

As soon as she finished emptying the cup she returned it to the box where he'd left it earlier, and lay down again – now on her side, her face to the wall with the blankets pulled snugly over her shoulders. A moment later her even breathing told him she was once again asleep.

Everything was considerably changed now. If she wasn't going to live out her remaining days as a vegetable he couldn't rightly return her just yet to her world. Both for her sake and his own he had to give her time to heal. If she healed enough maybe he could get her out here without having to carry her the entire way, making the trip a lot easier for himself physically – though with her broken leg he may still have to carry her much of the time and the going would be slow even if she did walk.

But there were two much more vital reasons for waiting, reasons that were of life and death importance for them both. First, of course, was her safety. Clearly if she was to return to her world in her present condition she would not be able to defend herself against a second attack. But if she was to improve steadily as it now looked like she might, fear of reprisal would likely force her attacker to take measures to prevent her ever revealing the events that had taken place there at the top of the bluff. To take her back now was a sure signing of her death warrant and would mean he had saved her life in vain.

Nor was he forgetting the danger to himself. His freedom depended on anonymity. If she was to return to the world in her present state there was every likelihood that, upon remembering what had happened to her, she would come searching for him. If she should remember his role in saving her she may wish to return just to thank him. But if not, if she should forget seeing him, would curiosity as to how she had gotten from the sight of her attack to safety, through three days and nights, not prompt her to come searching for the missing days of her life? Such a search would inevitably trap him without any means of escape.

But if she should be recovered when he took her back, if she should remember the attack and be made fully aware of his role in saving her life, surely her gratitude would prompt her to keep his secret. At least he should be able to judge her attitude enough to know what kind of threat her knowledge of him represented so he could take appropriate measures.

So he waited. While she slept he worked – washing up his breakfast dishes, chopping wood, carrying water, washing out his clothes, tending to his garden.

And still she slept.

Having finished his daily chores, he turned his attention to the beehive in the hollow of a tree a couple hundred yards from the cabin. Honey was his only source of sweetener, and he used the beeswax for the candles that were his only source of light in the cabin after dark.

It was an involved process. He first had to build a fire outside the hive to smoke the bees out so that he could reach inside the relatively small opening to remove the honeycomb without destroying the nest any more than he had to. Even with the smoke he managed to get himself stung twice, but there was a certain satisfaction in attaining his prize nonetheless.

Mud was just the thing for easing the pain of the stings, so he carried the bucket of dripping honeycomb the twenty yards to the stream running off the spring where he applied a thick layer of it to each of the stings, then washed the smoke from his face and arms.

As he sat there washing up his thoughts turned, as usual of late, to his guest. Was she still sleeping? Just how alert would she be the next time she awoke? Maybe he should check on her again, just in case she had taken a turn for the worst. Or maybe she was hungry by now. After all, it was near dinner time and she had eaten nothing since he'd found her.

His thoughts on his guest, he became aware of a bunch of wild, purple pansies growing around him as he retrieved his honey bucket. That was what she needed. Flowers were always brought to recovering patients. Maybe fresh flowers would cheer her enough to speed her recovery, and the sooner she recovered, the better.

Rather than just picking the flowers, he dug around the roots of two of the small plants, carrying them back to the cabin whole on a piece of bark to preserve as much of their soil as possible. They would live longer that way and stay fresher.

So it was with a bucket of honeycomb in one hand and a slab of bark containing two pansy plants in the other that he entered the cabin to find his guest wide awake again. This time, however, she was not in bed, but was standing in front of the stove wearing only his shirt with the tail ripped off. Standing on one bare foot, her splinted leg used only as balance, she was busy adding a stick of wood to the fire.

For a moment he could do nothing but stand there stupidly staring at the picture she made. Even dressed as she was, with the makeshift bandage covering much of her head, she was incredibly beautiful. Until that moment he hadn't noticed just how delicately beautiful she was. Of course, this was the first time he'd seen her on her feet in a pose that was so thoroughly domestic.

"Flowers," she said, turning to him with the most exquisite smile he'd ever seen. "You brought me flowers. That is so sweet."

Even her eyes smiled at him and all he could do was stutter.

"Flowers, yes," he said stupidly as he held them out to her on their tree-bark tray.

"Thank you," she said, taking them from him with a natural grace despite the physical hindrance of her bad leg. "That is so thoughtful. I must pot them quickly."

Like a half-witted imbecile he just stood there with his honey bucket watching her search for a suitable container to pot her pansies. When she settled on an rusty, old dipper he had never bothered trying to scrub clean enough to use, yet had not throw out since it had come with the cabin and thus did not belong to him, he was intrigued by her choice.

"May I use this?" she asked for his permission.

"Yes, of course," he agreed, surprised by the question. "If you think it'll work."

"It will work," she assured him with that same sweet smile, and he watched as she made it work quite well.

The dipper was large, such as was often used in generations past when drinking water was served in a bucket, shared by the entire family from a common dipper. It's size was sufficient to pot both plants together whereupon she packed the loose dirt remaining on the bark tray around them. Then, with a small amount of water from the bucket on the table she moistened the soil before hobbling over to hang the dipper on a large nail protruding from the wall by the window next to the bed.

"Thank you, she said again as she surveyed her work, then turned to give him another smile. "They are so beautiful."

Now that she was looking at him so directly he felt extremely self-conscious and, to ease that feeling, he turned his attention to setting the bucket down on the table as an excuse to turn his back to her.

"Are you hungry?" he asked.

"Starving," she said. "I was going to make dinner, but I wasn't sure what there was to fix."

"I'll fix dinner," he shrugged. "Maybe you should get back in bed and rest."

"Yes, rest," she said. "I am tired. And my whole body hurts. What happened to me?"

He turned to face her. "You don't remember?"

Her face was blank. It didn't appear that not remembering bothered her, but clearly she had no memory of her attack.

"No," she said. "I guess I should rest. My head is very foggy."

With the innocence of an obedient child she climbed back into bed and only a moment later was sleeping peacefully, all thought of dinner completely forgotten.

It was growing dark when the young woman awoke again, and her first thought was that she was hungry. To her delight a plate of fried meat and potatoes was waiting for her on the box where the cup of water had been earlier. So, without a thought about who this man was who had left it for her, she sat back to enjoy it.

As her head was still foggy no real thoughts were going through her mind. Instinct was her only motivating force. When she had been cold earlier, instinct had driven her to add fuel to the fire. When she was thirsty, she had instinctively consumed the water available to her. It was the same instinct that prompted her to consume the food she saw in front of her. She was hungry, so she ate. Even tending the flowers had been instinctive. They had needed cared for, so she had taken care of them.

When she was finished eating a new instinct took over – the instinct to use the bathroom. She didn't think about it, she didn't wonder where it was. She just went in search of it.

Being that the cabin had only one door she went through it. A path was clearly visible to her left so she hobbled along it. A tiny little house with a crescent shaped hole in the door appeared before her so she went inside.

Once finished tending to her instinctive needs she hobbled a little further along the path, no clear aim in mind, just an instinct for exploration. The path was there so she took it, finding herself a moment later at the edge of a beautiful spring, a stream flowing peacefully out of one side.

A bath, that was what she wanted. The water was so inviting she walked right in, heedless of the splint and the bandages, though some instinct made her remove the shirt to keep it from getting wet.

The water was cold, shockingly so. But that fact seemed not to penetrate the fogginess of her mind. She knew only the pleasure of feeling clean again after days without bathing.

"Are you trying to catch pneumonia?"

Her eyes turned at the sound of the voice to see the nice man who had given her the water and the food and the pretty flowers.

"Hello," she said with the innocent smile of a child. "I'm taking a bath."

"What you're doing is getting your bandages and your splint wet," he said in a hard tone, scowling fiercely. "And if you catch pneumonia you're on your own. I am not a nurse."

He turned his back, walking away from her, and her instincts again took over, causing her to hurry out of the water, grabbing up the shirt in passing without any self-consciousness.

"Are you angry with me?" she asked from behind him as she hobbled in his wake.

For the briefest instant he turned to face her as he started to answer, but her unashamed nakedness stopped him and he turned quickly away again.

"Put the shirt on," he snapped at her. She did so with the haste of a child eager to please a parent after an abrupt reprimand.

"I'm sorry," she said, following as he again walked away. "I didn't mean to make you angry. I won't do it any…"

The ground being uneven under her bare feet, in her haste, with her leg in the splint, she stumbled, suddenly putting too much weight on her bad leg. With a cry of pain she fell to a heap on the ground.

"I'm sorry," she sobbed, clutching the source of her pain as he turned back to see what had happened to her. "I didn't mean to be bad."

With a sigh he lifted her in his arms and carried her back to the cabin.

"I'm sorry," she repeated through mournful tears two or three more times.

"It's okay."

He laid her back on the bed, adding, "I'm not mad at you."

"Really?" she asked, begging childishly for reassurance.

"Really," he promised. "But I do want you to stay right here until I come back. Will you do that for me?"

He spoke to her as if she was the child she seemed to think she was, and he waited for her promise to do his bidding before he left to find dry splint sticks and bandage material. By the time he returned only moments later she was again fast asleep.

With a sigh he began removing the splint and the wet bandages. Even though she was asleep he knew they had to be replaced to prevent further damage to her wounds and irritation to her skin. It was also important to keep her dry and warm to prevent sickness, so he wrapped her again in the blankets. The last thing he needed was for this child/woman to get sick. She was enough trouble as it was.

When the young woman awoke again the morning sun was shining in at the uncovered window and she was alone. For several minutes she sat there on the bed just looking around. Her mind seemed clearer this morning, though that wasn't a conscious thought on her part. She knew only the familiarity of the room around her and the tranquil peace such familiarity brought her.

She remembered nothing beyond the cabin and her kind benefactor. The attack on her life, the life she'd known before it, even her own name – none of them were memories she could draw on. But not knowing, not remembering, did not register in her mind as a problem. She was happy here. Nothing else mattered.

Because her mind was clearer, the childish reflexes and reactions were fading as more mature ones surfaced. Her whole countenance was changed from the day before, though there was still in her an innocence stemming from a lack of remembered experience.

The first thing on her agenda for the day was the use of the outhouse. She remembered where it was so, beyond that dictated by the splint on her leg, there was no hesitation in her manner now as she opened the door to go to it. The kind man was chopping wood as she exited the cabin and she made a detour to say good morning to him first.

"Good morning," he acknowledged.

"Should I help you?" she asked.

"I can manage."

He sounded surly, but she didn't notice.

"I'll go to the bathroom then," she said and went off to do just that.

"There's water in the cabin for washing up," he said a few minutes later as she exited the outhouse.

"Okay," she acknowledged. "I won't go swimming again."

He stood watching as she walked back to the cabin, stopping midway between him and the door as a thought hit her. "What's your name?"

There was a long hesitation before he answered her question. "Mike," he said finally.

"Mike." She rolled the name off her tongue a couple of times, then gave him a smile. "I won't forget." And she left him staring after her as she turned once again and went inside.

When Mike carried his load of wood inside to pile it in the box near the stove, he found her standing at the stove heating a bit of animal fat in the skillet.

"I was going to make breakfast," she said. "But I can't find any food."

"The traps were empty this morning," he said as he dropped the wood into the box. "There's some rabbit left from yesterday if you want it and I can try and find some eggs or something."

"Are there any more potatoes?" she asked, remembering the ones he had served her the day before.

"You want potatoes?" he asked.

"If there are some I could cook them while you get the eggs," she suggested.

"There's some in the cellar."

Moving to the center of the room, he opened a trap door she had not previously noticed, and she hobbled over to peer down into the darkness below.

"The food is down there?" she asked.

"What there is of it," he said.

Being familiar with the cellar, he didn't bother lighting a candle to take with him. The light above was enough to get him by, and a moment later he was climbing back into the room with three nice-sized potatoes and the remainder of the rabbit from the day before, already cooked and stored in a large covered bowl.

Handing the food supplies to her he closed the trap door. "I'll see about some eggs," he added before leaving the cabin.

Carefully she scrubbed the potatoes, then minced them and the meat into the smallest pieces she could manage with the available knife, and started them frying together in the hot grease. By the time Mike returned with the two pale-green eggs she had some nicely browned hash ready to serve.

As there was only one plate and one bowl in the whole cabin, he watched as she used both of them to serve the hash before scrambling the eggs in the skillet. While they cooked she poured some water into the cup and placed it next to the plate on the table. Then, as soon as the eggs were finished she divided them between the plate and the bowl as well and took her place in front of the bowl with the spoon in hand to eat her breakfast.

Mike said nothing as he took the place she'd left for him in front of the plate. But he found it hard not to stare at her as he ate in silence the breakfast she'd provided him with. Apparently she saw nothing unusual about this place or the circumstances in which she found herself. The lack of electricity or running water, the meager and very basic provisions, her scant clothing – none of it seemed to concern her at all. It was as if she knew only this world, that she had never seen another, that her life had begun with her waking in his cabin and was thus all perfectly natural to her.

"Can you tell me your name?" he asked finally.

"My name is…"

For a second he thought he had been wrong about her, that she did know her name and that she was going to give it to him. But then her eyes narrowed as she tried to remember and failed.

"I guess not," she said without any real concern. "That's kind of funny, isn't it. But I guess I not have one. Do I need one?"

"Most people have names," he said, watching her.

Was it possible her inability to remember her name was just an act? Was it possible the reason she seemed so unconcerned by her lack of memory was that she did remember and was reluctant to reveal it to him? Had she recognized him? Was she only playing this game of innocence in an effort to protect herself from him, maybe from a ransom demand to her family or worse?

"What name should I have?" she asked. Her eyes were thoughtful. "I could be…"

Suddenly she was more serious than he had yet seen her. "Is it Penny?"

She seemed to be asking him for confirmation, as if the answer was suddenly of paramount importance. But he had no answer to give her.

"I don't know," he said when she continued looking at him. "Is it?"

Her eyes squinted nearly shut as she thought about it. "I think it is," she said after a moment. "I wonder why I didn't know that before. Hmm."

Mike was no psychologist, but he debated whether or not to tell her what he knew about her as she returned to eating. If she did know who he was, perhaps an open and honest disclosure on his part would make her feel more comfortable. She wouldn't have to wonder what he was up to or what he might intend to do with her.

But he couldn't believe this was just an act. She seemed perfectly content and relaxed. If she did recognize him, surely her fear of him would show in her face. At the very least she would be concerned about his part in her attack. Having been struck from behind by her companion it was only logical, now that she was here alone with him, that she would assume he had struck her and maybe her companion as well. Unless she'd had some previous reason to suspect her companion capable of such an attack – which was unlikely since she had allowed herself to be taken so completely by surprise – she would be concerned with her companion's safety as well.

But there was no sign of fear or even nervousness in her eyes or her manner whatsoever. Nor had she made any attempt to accost him unawares or to make an escape. To all indications she was an amnesiac without a care in the world.

Yet she had come up with a name – Penny. Was that her name? Had she remembered something so simple as her name? Or had she just made one up to appease him? If it was a memory, was it a real one? Or was it some odd trick of a broken memory that remembered something completely irrelevant and had only connected it to herself?

Real or not, would there be more? Would she gradually remember other details about herself? And how many? Would she remember her attack and her attacker? Would she be aware of the actual events that had brought her into his life? Or would her confused mind find him guilty of crimes he had not committed? And how was he to know the best time – both for himself and for her – to return her to her world?

"How does your head feel?" he asked.

"My head?"

Her hand went up to encounter the bandage that covered it, seemingly surprised by its presence.

"Is something wrong with my head?"

"You've had a pretty bad bump on it," he said, watching her thoughtful eyes as her hand continued to probe the bandage.

"It doesn't hurt," she said. Apparently she was puzzled by his need to even ask such a question.

"I guess it's healing well, then," he said. "How about your leg?"

"My leg," she said, looking down at it. "It hurts. When I walk it hurts more."

"Maybe you should avoid walking so much," he suggested.

"Okay," she agreed without compulsion.

For several minutes he just watched her eat. Her eyes wandered after a moment, eventually settling on the dipper of pansies on the wall. The conversation was forgotten as she smiled softly toward them. They seemed to give her genuine pleasure, but suddenly he felt uncomfortable for no good reason that he could think of.

"Thanks for breakfast," he said, getting abruptly to his feet. "I've got work to do."

She made no comment as he departed. But her gentle smile followed him from the room.

Mike spent the entire morning outside, finding one thing after another to occupy his time. His guest was feeling much better now. She didn't need him checking up on her any more, and he just wouldn't waste his time doing so.

Perhaps an hour after he left her, a gunshot coming from the north side of the cabin suddenly echoed through the quiet of the forest. Instantly Mike was alert. It sounded like the squirrel gun he'd left hanging in its usual place over the door, but he couldn't be certain. Even if it was his gun, caution was essential. Whatever Penny – he found the name came naturally to his mind, that it fit her well – whatever Penny was up to, a gun in her hands could be a dangerous thing.

There was only the one shot, and he was in a position to see the cabin a moment later when she came hobbling around the side of the cabin with his gun in one hand and a rabbit hanging from its hind legs in the other. Rather than entering the cabin again, though, he saw her sit on the stump beside the outhouse, lay the gun down at her feet, and begin skinning and gutting her catch with an expert hand, using the knife from the cabin that he always used.

All he could do was watch in awe. Whoever this woman was, she was obviously able to fend for herself. The skill she showed in preparing that rabbit came with practice, and the fact she'd used only one shot to hit her target also spoke of experience. He was going to have to watch himself around her so long as she had possession of his gun. That was certain.

When she was finished with the rabbit she carried it and the gun inside, but she was back in just a minute to carry the remains of her catch into the woods for disposal before returning to the cabin and closing the door.

So, he thought as he returned to his work, they would be having rabbit again for lunch. That wasn't unusual for him. Rabbit, squirrel, trout, possum, snake, pheasant – those were the staples of his diet. But he found himself looking forward to lunch all the same, curious to see what she did with it.

Despite the fact that he still wore the watch he'd worn since before his arrest, time normally meant nothing to him. Having been alone for so long he relied more on his body's internal clock than he did on the actual time itself. If he was hungry he ate, if he was tired he slept, when he woke up he got up. But today, for some reason, he kept thinking of lunch all morning, and it was only the fact that his watch indicated noon was a long way off that kept him from returning before then.

Precisely at twelve o'clock, though, he came in through the door. An almost overpoweringly appetizing aroma hit his nostrils before he'd even set foot inside, and he could see the source of the wonderful smells was the pot in which he usually kept water heating on the stove. It was filled to nearly bubbling over with a thick rabbit and vegetable stew.

As he opened the door Penny was sitting at the table with a piece of wood and his knife in her hands, but immediately on spotting him she put them down and got to her feet.

"Are you hungry?" she asked.

"Starved," he admitted.

There was something companionable about her smile as she filled his bowl with her stew, something homey and comfortable in having her wait on him. It was such a long time since he'd had any human companionship, and now this strange woman was here caring for him, serving him in a way that was both comforting and frightening at the same time.

As he sat down to the meal which she provided for him, she reached past him to pick up something, a second bowl. His eyes jumped to her face as he realized it was a bowl she had carved from a piece of wood. Crude though it was, it would clearly serve its purpose. She'd made a spoon as well.

"You made that?" he asked stupidly.

"I know it's not very good," she said, apology in her voice and in her eyes. "But this way we won't have to keep sharing. And you said I shouldn't walk too much. But you're always working so hard, so I wanted to do something useful, too."

"It's great," he said. His sincerity brought the smile back to her face.

"I'm making a cup right now," she said, indicating the project she'd held in her hands on his arrival. "And then I was going to make a plate and a fork. But my hand is getting rather tired of this right now. I think I'll rest it first."

He watched as she took her handmade bowl to fill with stew at the stove. There was something so amazingly different about this woman from any woman he had ever known. Even on her best days Diane would have thrown a fit at being confined in such a primitive place with no electricity, no running water, no local market to pick up the little conveniences, no gourmet restaurant just around the corner to satisfy that exotic palate of hers, only one of his shirts to wear day and night, no shoes, not even any underwear…

That thought made him suddenly look away from her. Allowing his thoughts to dwell on such intimate details was going to drive him crazy. If he was even to think of making a pass at Penny it would make her uncomfortable. Diane was right. No woman wanted a man like him touching her. And he was not ready to deal with the disgust he would see in her eyes or the mocking taunts she would hurl his way if he should even contemplate such actions.

"The stew is good," he said in an effort to focus his thoughts on something less stressful.

"Thank you."

She gave him a smile, but as he was still looking at his bowl of stew, he missed it. She didn't mind, though. He had praised her stew and her bowl. She was content.

The next few days came and went in a calm, comfortable manner that became routine. Penny and Mike both began their days with the rising of the sun and ended them at dusk – thus saving on candles. Penny seemed not to remember anything other than the little world she'd known since waking up in his cabin, but it didn't seem to matter to her. And Mike, not wanting to return her to her world until he knew she would be safe, did nothing to push her into wanting to go.

Penny took care of the cooking and cleaning inside the cabin, hobbling around until her leg began hurting her too much, then resting it while she carved more little items for the cabin, sometimes useful items like plates and forks, sometimes extra little items just for decoration that gave the place that feminine touch despite being so primitive. She seemed to take pride in making things comfortable and homey.

Mike kept her supplied with fresh meat from his traps and birds that he shot, or fish he caught in the stream. He also supplied the wood for the fire that she now tended and carried the water from the spring she used for cooking and cleaning. By the end of her first week with him he was also able to provide her with the first fresh lettuce from his garden, as well as small radishes and carrots he thinned out from among the others. It was a great change from the remnants of last season's crops in the cellar, and he felt a sense of pride at her apparent appreciation.

By then Penny was no longer sporting the bandages on her head and leg, though she still wore the splint. The wounds were healing nicely and, as she found the bandages uncomfortable, she saw no reason to wear them any longer.

They developed a routine for sharing his clothes. She still wore only his shirts, and occasionally a pair of socks if her feet were cold. Her meager wardrobe never seemed to bother her – maybe because her petite frame was so well covered by the length of his large shirts. But having only three shirts between them made it impossible for each to wear a fresh one each morning while washing and drying the used ones.

So they came up with a solution. First thing every morning Mike would, after bathing in the creek, wash out the clothes he'd been wearing and change into the only spare shirt. The now clean shirt he would hang near the stove with the other clothes he'd been wearing to dry until mid-afternoon when Penny would take her bath in the stream – careful now to keep her splint dry – and wash out the shirt she'd been wearing to hang by the stove in place of the one she now wore.

Most of each day Mike spent outdoors. He had chores to do, but he found himself inventing extra chores to do just because being inside with Penny made him uncomfortable. The more he got to know her the more remarkable he found her to be. She continued to remember nothing previous to her appearance in his life, but she was comfortable with her ignorance. It seemed not remembering had robbed her of the need to remember. Her world was here and now, and she cared nothing for the past.

Such ignorance gave Mike increasing concern. If she never remembered, would he be forced to keep her here indefinitely? Or did he have a moral obligation to return her to her world regardless of her ability to fend off a second attack on her life should one be made? Surely someone would be looking for her by now. Would they come looking for her here? He really doubted it. He knew her attacker had chosen this place for that very reason.

And yet, should someone come looking, he knew they would never believe any story he might give them about his innocence. With his record they would only tack on another twenty year sentence for attempting to take her life. Even if he could convince them he had saved her life, not tried to take it, they would never understand his keeping her here for so long.

And yet he couldn't bring himself to take her back until she was able to protect herself. Her companion had nearly succeeded in destroying her completely with this attempt. Without previous knowledge of that fact a second attempt would have no chance of failing.

At least that's what he told himself night after night as he slept on the floor. Having grown accustomed to the hard surface he slept well enough. But dreams of Diane came back regularly to haunt him, her taunting laughter, the scorn in her eyes during that last fight plaguing him as strongly as they had in the beginning. For some time now they had begun fading from his mind, but now that Penny was in his life, the anguish – the guilt and the pain – were back as strongly as ever. Diane was dead – he could still see her lying in her own blood at his feet – and yet she lived on in the nightmares that he feared would never stop haunting him.

Chapter Three

The ninth night after Penny's arrival at the cabin, the sixth since she'd first awakened, a storm began to brew. Mike saw it coming from the southwest by early evening, but it took three or four hours to reach them, bringing with it wild winds and rains. Because the sun had already gone down both Penny and Mike were in their respective beds. But, as the thunder rolling in the distance drew closer and closer to the cabin, Penny found herself growing more and more restless.

Strange thoughts filled her mind. Memories and half-memories mingled with nightmares both past and present. She didn't bother trying to determine which were which, or to make sense of any of them. She knew only that, silly as it was to let a little thunder make her so nervous, she could not control the terrors that grew within her.

It's only noise, she told herself over and over again. There is nothing to worry about. But she was not easily convinced.

"Are you okay?" Mike asked as a particularly close clap of thunder caused her to jump visibly in her bed, forcing a muffled cry from her throat.

"Yes, I'm okay," she said quickly. "I'm sorry I disturbed you."

Rain was beating fiercely on the roof now and she tried to concentrate on that. Rain was harmless, even rain that was pouring so hard, pounding so loudly on the roof. But, as another clap of thunder seemed to hit right outside the window she let out another startled cry and pulled the blanket up over her head.

"If it would help we can light a candle," Mike suggested.

Penny forced herself to relax. The last thing she wanted to do was upset Mike, and he'd already made it clear that candles were scarce. They couldn't afford to waste one now just because she was being so childish.

"I'm okay," she said again.

As the next clap of thunder echoed through the darkness she clapped her hands over her mouth to prevent herself from crying out. It was only noise, only noise–

The movement of Mike getting up from his bed on the floor caught her attention and guilt bit at her for disturbing him. But she said nothing as he walked across to the woodpile where he pulled a long sliver from a stick of firewood. As he opened the stove, lit the sliver, then used it as a match to light a candle, she felt the guilt grow.

"Maybe this will help," he said as he handed it to her.

She wanted to assure him that she was just fine, she didn't need the light he offered. It was too dim to really be much help anyway, and yet the kindness of his efforts did make her feel better.

"Thank you."

The heartfelt words touched him, and for a moment he just stared down at the deep, dark eyes that stared up at him. But, as his thoughts made him suddenly nervous, he turned away to return to his hard, cold bed on the floor.

Lack of human companionship had made a mental case out of him, he decided. If he hadn't been so deprived of company for so long he wouldn't be having this insane craving in the pit of his stomach. The desire to hold her close was only a result of his being so alone for so long. And she would only despise him if he acted on that need. His very need would alienate her completely.

"Mike?"

Her voice was soft and timid, as if she was afraid she was bothering him.

"What?"

"I'm sorry," she said. "Thunderstorms just make me so nervous. When I was a kid lightning struck a tree just in front of our car as we were driving down the road. The tree was on fire as it fell in front of us and Daddy couldn't stop in time. We hit the tree pretty hard, totaled the car–"

She hesitated as the picture of that event played so vividly in her mind, the terror she'd felt that day so long ago still possessing the power to transport her back to that place and time.

"You remember that?" he asked into the silence of the moment that followed.

"I wish I didn't," she said as another thunderbolt crashed through the night. But it was a moment before she realized the significance of that fact.

"Mike?" she said after another minute, sitting up in the bed as her thoughts became more intense.

"Hmm?" His thoughts were at the moment on the progress of her memory. This was the first real sign that she was remembering anything, and he found himself wondering just how much more there would be.

"Why is it I remember some things – like the cabin, and being afraid of thunderstorms – but I can't seem to remember you or what happened to my leg?"

"You remember the cabin?"

How could she remember the cabin? he puzzled. Had she really been here before? Was that why she was so comfortable here? The place had seemed so abandoned when he'd first arrived, and in the year he'd been here she was the first person he'd seen near it. But could she have been here before that? If so, would someone think to come looking for her now? Was he to be caught after all?

"It seems different somehow," she said. "But I remember it. All the summer vacations and Christmas vacations and spring breaks we spent here–"

Could she be remembering another cabin and confusing the two? Or had she only come here as a child and no one had been here since she had grown up – at least not in the year since his arrival?

"But what happened to me?" she asked in a subdued tone as she stared at the candle in her hands, apparently having forgotten the thunder now that it was not quite so near and her thoughts were so centered on her memories. "What happened to my leg, and my head? What am I doing here? I don't remember coming to the cabin this time. And why are you here instead of my father? Why don't I remember you?"

Still clutching her candle, she turned her dark eyes to him, and in the light that flickered softly on her face, he saw for the first time the look of a person lost and confused. The time had come. He had to tell her all he knew. And yet, he wondered, was she ready to hear that a woman she had trusted had so deviously and viciously tried to erase her very life?

"Mike? Please?" she begged in a whisper that touched him deeply.

"This is where I live," he said finally, unsure just how to tell her what she needed to know. "You'd been...injured. I found you and brought you here until you're well enough to go home."

"You mean...this is your cabin? Not ours?"

He gave her no answer. He couldn't. He had no real knowledge of who the cabin did belong to, and to say differently may just complicate things.

"Mike, I am so sorry," she said. "You don't even know me, do you? I just moved in...eating your food...and you gave me your bed?!"

That last thought caused her to swing her legs over the side of the bed. The storm, as it moved off into the distance, was forgotten as guilt hit her.

"I should be sleeping down there. This is your..."

"Don't be ridiculous," he snapped.

His tone was sharp, and it stopped her instantly. The last thing she wanted to do was anger him after all his kindness.

"I'm sorry, Mike," she said again. "I had no idea I was intruding. If you will point me in the right direction I'll get out of your way first thing in the morning."

"And how do you propose to do that?" he demanded. "It's more than a mile to the nearest road, and who knows how many miles to civilization from there. How far do you think you'd get in that splint? And if you think I'm carrying you out of here you are sadly mistaken."

For a long moment she just sat there staring at him, and guilt for speaking so abruptly to her made him turn onto his side facing away from her so that he wouldn't have to see the worried look flickering on her face in the candlelight. It seemed an eternity before he heard her blow out the candle, sending the room again into complete darkness, and then crawl back into bed.

The thunder could still be heard faintly in the distance, but no longer was she jumping or crying out at the sound. Even so, he was aware as he lay there in the dark, that she did not go to sleep.

"Penny?" he called softly into the silence when he could stand it no longer. "I'm sorry. You just can't go home right now. But I promise, when you're stronger, I'll help you get home. Okay?"

"Thank you," she said quietly. Then after a moment, as if the idea had just hit her, she added, "Mike, did you...save my life?"

"I guess I did," he said.

"Thank you for that, too," she said. "I'll always be grateful to you for that. And, Mike, if there is anything I can do for you–"

"I'll let you know," he promised. "Goodnight."

"Goodnight, Mike," she said. "And thank you for the candle, too."

He mumbled a reply and she was silent, not wanting to disturb him further, and a moment later she was asleep.

Penny stood in the middle of a beautiful meadow, surrounded on all sides by the vibrant colors of spring. In the distance in every direction all that could be seen were the oak-covered hills in all their spender – the dogwoods and redbuds bringing their bright spring beauty to the green of the oaks, the occasional pine poking it's top up from among the hardwoods.

Birds sang, the sun was warm and cheerful, the breeze cool and light. Squirrels and rabbits bounded playfully through the meadow around her. An eagle soared lazily overhead. A doe and fawn grazed unconcerned at the edge of the clearing. All was peaceful and right with the world.

Just ahead of her was the cabin. The open door and the light smoke rising from it's chimney were inviting, and cheerfully she danced through the flowers at her feet to reach it's warmth.

Suddenly it changed. No longer was it the cabin she saw before her, but a house, large and white, a new oak swing hanging from the roof of the huge, covered porch across the front. Tall and proud the house stood there, and it, too, invited her in.

She loved this house. It was her home. All the years of her childhood had been spent right here – happy, fun-filled years with the people she loved. And they were all here – her father and mother, Becky and Susie, Peter and David, Aunt Nancy and Uncle Joe, Uncle Bob and Aunt Sally, Grandma and Grandpa Baker, Grandma Loftin, even her friends – Caroline, and Tina, and Julia and Steve. And, yes, there was Robert, Robert who loved her, Robert who wanted to marry her.

She hurried toward them all, eager to see them, eager to be with the people who loved her and whom she adored in return. They were all so happy to see her as she joined them. Daddy hugged her, Mama held her tight for a long emotional moment, tears of joy filling her eyes. Caroline and Tina and Julia all hugged her, as did her sisters, Becky and Susie, even her brothers. Everyone was so happy for her, their congratulations heartfelt and sincere.

And there was Robert. The ring he slipped on her finger was beautiful – extravagant, but incredibly beautiful. And then he was kissing her to seal the promise of his love and they were alone. Penny was so happy. Robert loved her. He wanted to marry her. Everyone was so happy for her.

Then suddenly everything changed. Robert was still there, and he was still kissing someone, but it wasn't Penny. She was there in his arms, but it was not her mouth that he was kissing. She backed away and saw the other woman in her place. She could not see the face of the woman who had stolen Robert's affections from her, but she hated her immediately, wanting to claw her eyes out at the anger and frustration she felt.

But, as she protested the betrayal of her trust, the woman hid behind Robert and he denied her existence. Penny could no longer see the woman, Robert was hiding her, but she knew she was still there, and the woman laughed at her unmercifully.

There was only one thing to do in the face of Robert's betrayal. The ring on her finger had turned ugly and she was glad to remove it from her finger to drop it at his feet. He protested that he loved her, that it was all a mistake, but only on the surface. When she turned away from him, he was glad to retrieve the ring she'd dropped to place it on the finger of the other woman. And, as Penny buried her face in her hands, sobbing miserably, their haunting laughter echoed through her head and her heart.

How could they have done this to her? she sobbed. Robert, who loved her and wanted to marry her – how could he have betrayed her so deeply? But her sobs only deepened as she could find no answers.

"Penny?"

There was kindness in the voice that spoke to her, but it did not fully penetrate her consciousness.

"Penny?" The kind voice tried again. "You're dreaming, Penny. Come on, wake up."

It took several seconds for the kindness in that tone to penetrate the sadness of her dream, but when a gentle finger caressed her tear-stained cheek she knew a needed comfort, and her arms went instinctively around the neck of the man offering it to her.

"Why did he have to do that to me?" she sobbed into his shoulder.

"Who, Penny?" the voice asked softly as two hesitant arms caressed her and held her close. "Why did who do what?"

"Robert," she sobbed. "Oh, Daddy, why did he betray me? He said he loved me. Why did I believe him?"

The arms stiffened as she called him Daddy. She didn't know who he was. When she realized her mistake she would regret turning to him. Yet, when he tried to release her she clung to him so tightly he could not remove her arms from his neck without force.

"I gave him back his ring," she said. "I told him I can't marry him."

Her tone indicated the need for approval of her actions and he gave it.

"You did the right thing," he said. "If he betrayed your love you cannot marry him."

"But it hurts," she sobbed in his arms. "Oh, Daddy, it hurts so much."

"Of course it does," he said.

He understood that pain. He understood all too well the heartache of betrayal that stabbed deep beyond the heart to the very soul. It was a pain he had not forgotten in two years, a pain that would haunt him forever.

"I know it hurts," he said, more to himself than to her. "It hurts a lot. It hurts deep."

"You're not mad that I gave him back his ring?" she asked through her tears.

"No, Penny," he said. "You cannot marry a man who has betrayed you."

"No," she said. "I can't marry him." And that seemed to help her relax. Her sobs slowed almost immediately, and soon he knew she was asleep in his arms.

For a long, long time he just held her, needing her closeness as comfort for his own pain. In all this time, since the moment Diane had laughed so cruelly in his face – betraying the love she had vowed always to give him – he had never known comfort. No one had understood his pain. No one had cared. Even Joe, his brother – the one person who had stood by him throughout the trial – had not fully understood his pain. How could he without having shared it, without experiencing the tearing of his soul?

No one had held him then. No one had shared even the briefest hug to warm his heart, to make him feel just the tiniest bit less alone. And he had been alone even then, even out there in the world that had once been his, before coming to the isolation of this cabin.

But now he had someone. Granted she did not know or understand his pain. She was unaware even of the circumstances that had led to and followed his pain, and in the morning she was going to resent having turned to him in her distress. But tonight, for the first time in two years, he felt the comfort of being close to another human being, and he could not stop the tears that burned his eyes, nor bring himself to release her for a long, long time.

Penny was subdued and withdrawn the next morning, and Mike could easily understand why. First he had snapped at her for suggesting she take his place on the floor or that she leave him in the morning. Then he had allowed her to confess her pain to him as she'd sobbed in his arms. He'd held her when he had no right to do so – him a man who had no right to touch any woman.

As he awoke at first light he saw her looking at him with a strangely serious look in her face, and when immediately she looked away he knew she resented him. To ease her discomfort he quickly rose and left the cabin. He wouldn't force her to endure his presence any more than necessary.

After the things she'd said last night he was certain she was beginning to remember her life, though there was nothing to indicate she remembered what had happened to bring her here. Nor could he see a connection between the two events and the two people he now knew about. Robert and the woman with her on that cliff. One had betrayed her in love, the other had betrayed her by trying to take her life.

Robert. She had been engaged to a man named Robert, a man who had assuredly promised to love her. Yet he had betrayed her love – Mike assumed with another woman. But surely if the woman involved in that betrayal had been the woman on the cliff who had attempted to take her life, Penny would never have trusted that woman in such a situation – coming for a drive to such an isolated place, turning her back on the woman in a place that could offer her no protection.

So still he knew nothing about that woman or her motives, and he was not about to stir up Penny's pain by bringing up a subject she apparently still did not remember.

But Penny did remember. Remembering Robert had triggered a chain of memories that ended on the cliff. As the morning progressed one thought led to another until every detail of her life was as clear as it had been before her attack. But even knowing all she did, she was no closer to understanding what had happened to her than was Mike who had no knowledge of the situation. One minute she was standing with her friend admiring the view, the next something hard and heavy hit her on the back of the head and everything went black.

Never for a second did Penny entertain the thought that Mike might have been involved in that blow as he worried she might do after finding herself alone with him in his cabin. Even at the moment it was happening she had been aware – too late – what Caroline had done.

"Sorry, Penny."

The words had echoed through her brain in that moment as darkness had come over her. Caroline, her trusted friend, had struck her unconscious. Being unconscious she was unaware of all that had taken place after that blow, but apparently it had been a lot for her to have broken her leg and been scratched up so badly.

And she was now wearing one of Mike's shirts rather than the blue jeans and cotton shirt she had been wearing. It never entered her mind to accuse Mike of having harmed her in any way or removed her clothing. He was the one who had found her injured body, who had given her the shirt off his back, something she knew to be a sacrifice on his part. She never once suspected him of anything but genuine kindness.

But Caroline? What could have prompted her to make such an attack on a friend? They had been friends since grade school – despite their differences. While Caroline had always been popular – outgoing and strikingly beautiful – Penny had been plainer and shy. And, though both had grown up in affluent homes, Penny with her two brothers and two sisters had always lived a rather reserved life in comparison to Caroline's easily spoiled, only-child youth.

Often over the years Penny had suspected that their friendship was based more on the fact that she felt sorry for Caroline and that Caroline craved the love Penny's family had always shown each other, rather than on any real fondness between them.

Naturally, as with any two friends, they'd had their differences over the years. But whenever Penny was upset or unhappy – whether at losing one of the few boyfriends she'd had in school or losing out on the coveted spot on the cheerleading team – Caroline was always there to cheer her up. And when Caroline was hurting because of her parent's divorce or the death of her first real love during their first year of college, it was Penny's shoulder on which she cried.

For a long time after Brian's death Penny had suspected his passing had affected Caroline more than she let on. She was moody and accusing, angry and cruel at times, and her spoiled tantrums grew to an almost intolerable level for a time, though she seemed to have worked her way through that now. But even with all of that, Penny found it difficult to believe her capable of the cold-blooded murder of her best friend.

What had prompted such behavior? It wasn't completely out of character for her to be vindictive and spoiled. Even to be violent, Penny realized, was not totally unexpected. But even she would have had to have had a reason for such behavior, and Penny could think of no possible reason for her to turn so abruptly on their friendship.

Since graduating from college their friendship had grown closer than ever. Penny had gone to work for her father where her older brother, David was already working, while Caroline had been pleased not to have to work at all – that her allowance was sufficient to keep her living in her present lifestyle without taking up her time or her energies in working for her money.

She had seemed perfectly content with her carefree life. She did what she wanted, when she wanted, without restraint or responsibility. If she wanted to date a doctor or a lawyer she did so. If she preferred a lowly laborer or an artist or an exotic dancer she had no difficulty in finding one to make her happy.

It was far from the life Penny would have wanted, but Caroline had seemed contented. She had everything she wanted – a brand new Ferrari, an expensive condo, furs, men, the time and money to live as she chose. And she had never shown any sign of jealousy or discontent with Penny over anything. After all, what did Penny have in comparison – a ten year old Tempo, a moderate apartment, she worked for her living, even Robert, the man she had once planned to marry had been an insignificant business man whom Caroline had not even particularly liked.

There was no logical reason at all for Caroline to attack her that way, and yet she had, and throughout the day Penny fretted over why. "Sorry, Penny," she'd said as she'd brought that blow down on her head. Had she expected her to die out here alone and naked. It seemed likely, though in Caroline's mind there was a possibility she had only intended keeping her out of the way for a while for some crazy reason. It could even have been a spontaneous impulse as she often hit out at people and things as some frustrating thought bothered her.

And yet she had said she was sorry. That wasn't consistent with anything Penny knew about her, as if she had thought about her actions in advance and, while she regretted them, had felt she had no choice. Not knowing her motives, though, was both confusing and frightening.

That fear concerned her as nothing else ever had because it left her with a dilemma. Now that Caroline had removed her from the picture what else had she done? How had she explained Penny's disappearance? Had she even made an explanation? So far as Penny knew no one even knew they had been together that afternoon. Caroline had begged her to go for a drive and she had gone without saying anything to anyone. There had been no reason to say anything when she had left her own apartment to spend a Sunday afternoon with a friend.

But what had Caroline expected to accomplish? A part of Penny wanted to return home immediately to find out what it was all about, to ease the concern her family was sure to be feeling at her disappearance. Yet another part of her dreaded returning, dreaded facing a friend who had left her here to die.

If not for Mike she most certainly would have died, she was certain of that. Though she was unaware of just how critical her condition had been, she knew it must have been serious indeed for her to have gone for so long without remembering even who she was. Days had passed, she had no idea how many, and yet, despite the inconvenience to himself, Mike had continued to care for her, saving her life, sharing his meager provisions with her, even giving up his bed for her.

She owed him more than she could ever repay, and it looked like she was going to owe him even more before she was through. He was right, even if she was sure she wanted to go home right now, she couldn't get there without his help. Not only would it be next to impossible with her broken leg which ached after only short periods of standing or walking around the cabin, but she had no idea which way was out.

And last night she had cried in his arms like a child after the nightmare that had reminded her of Robert – Robert who had betrayed her love so cruelly. In her distress she had thought he was her father, and it was humiliating to think she had clung to him so childishly. Yet he had not taken advantage of her for a moment. She had felt only comfort in his arms until sleep had finally reclaimed her.

But clearly that episode of kindness had left him feeling uncomfortable. He already spent much of his time outdoors, but today he seemed to spend even more there. When he was in the house for meals or carrying in firewood and water he avoided looking directly at her, and she felt it was all her fault.

Did he sense the gratitude she felt toward him? Was he afraid her feelings might become more than that? Was he concerned that he not encourage feelings in her that he couldn't return?

He liked being alone, she was aware of that. He wouldn't have chosen to live so far from the rest of the world if he didn't. And now he avoided being inside the cabin with her as much as possible for the same reason. She was intruding in his private world. After all he had done for her she knew she owed it to him to return his privacy as soon as possible.

He didn't talk much, certainly not about himself. Except for his first name she really knew nothing about him at all. Yet she did know that he was kind, that he had saved her life, and for those reasons she was determined to make things as comfortable for him as she possibly could.

Making things more comfortable for him included not pressing him for conversation when he preferred to be left alone – even though there were so many things she wanted desperately to ask him about both himself and his rescuing her. Instead she contented herself with cooking and cleaning the best she could with what she had to work with, carving little things out of wood while she sat resting her foot, and trying to give Mike the space she felt he desired.

Rather than his growing more comfortable with her, though, he seemed to grow more and more restless and she felt certain that, had she been able to make the trip, he would have escorted her out of here long ago. The time had come. She had to convince him she was ready to go.

Before she left, however, she wanted to find a way to thank him properly for all he had done for her – rescuing her, caring for her needs, giving her his hospitality despite the insufficiency of his own meager possessions. To that end she began working on a gift she would create with her own hands just for him. She had nothing else to give him.

For two days she worked on his gift, keeping it a secret until the right moment. It wasn't difficult, as little time as he spent indoors she had plenty of time to work without him noticing. And, as she worked at the table next to the front window, she was always able to see him coming soon enough to have her project hidden under the bed before he opened the door.

There were times, though, when she was nearly caught, and at those times he would give her an odd look which, in her mind, was a suspicion about what she was up to, but which was, in reality, a concern that he had startled her and that she wished he would go away and leave her alone, something he was always quick to do.

When finally the gift was ready, the Saturday night two weeks after her attack – though she wasn't counting – she made special plans to present it to him. Because of wanting this night and this gift to accurately express her gratitude to him, she planned everything perfectly, and she was ready when he came in to dinner.

As was her usual fashion, she served dinner in silence – both the stew that he seemed fond of, and a fresh, simple salad with no dressing since she knew no way to make one with the available ingredients. As usual he asked for no conversation as he ate, and she did not disrupt his enjoyment of the meal by offering any, except to advise him that she had made desert.

Being the first time she had served him any form of desert she was slightly nervous as she anticipated his reaction to her dish of wild blackberries stewed with honey, but apparently he found it tasteful, because he had seconds. It was only as he appeared finished and ready to leave the table that she produced her gift, handing it to him without a word.

"What is this?" he demanded, his face hard, his voice stern as he looked it over.

"It's a hat," she said, nervous now in case he didn't like it.

"I can see it's a hat," he said, his thoughts unreadable behind the stern expression he wore.

"It's made of straw," she said, though he could easily see that for himself.

"You made this?"

She nodded nervously, though he was not looking at her so he wouldn't have seen it.

"What's it for?" he asked.

She wished she could determine how he felt about it, but if anything his expression became more unreadable.

"Well, I thought…well, summer is coming," she tried to explain. "It's going to start getting hot. And you don't have anything to keep the sun off your head and out of your eyes. I just…I thought you might like it."

She couldn't hide the uncertainty in her voice. She wanted to please him, but apparently, from the hard look on his face, she had done a poor job of it.

"Well, you shouldn't have gone to all this trouble," he said as impatiently he got to his feet. He hated her gift. After all her careful work he hated what she had done, and the disappointment she felt at that thought ripped through her like a knife.

Chapter Four

"I'm sorry, Mike," Penny said as he rose from the table, still not even looking at her, to stand in front of the stove staring down at the hat in his hands that she'd made for him. She could almost picture him opening the door to the stove and throwing her handiwork into the fire in his disgust with her so inadequate gift. "I only…I wanted to thank you."

When he said nothing, when he did nothing but stand there with his back to her she wanted to cry, to beg him to forgive her for whatever she had done to upset him with her gift.

"I'm sorry," she said again. "It's just…you saved my life. You've given me everything I have – a place to stay, first-aid, the food I eat, the clothes I wear, the bed I sleep in… I had nothing to give you in return, and I wanted to say thank you."

Still he did not turn to face her, though now he was fondling the straw hat as if he might actually find it appealing.

"I also wanted to say goodbye," she added.

He turned then. "Goodbye?"

His face was as hard as ever, his eyes boring through her with an expression she couldn't quite understand – hard, yet maybe a little sad as well.

"I'm going to leave in the morning," she said. "You won't have to take me. I'll be slow, but if you point me in the right direction I will make it."

"Why?"

The steely tone in that one word was so hard she felt bruised by his anger, anger she couldn't seem to comprehend. It was for him she was leaving, yet it seemed to irate him. Did he think she was going because she was ungrateful for all he had done? That was the farthest thing from the truth.

"Mike, I…I know you'd rather be alone," she said. "I know that's why you spend so much of your time outside to avoid me. This is your home. And you've been so kind to me, if I go now you'll be able to enjoy your home again without me bothering you any more."

He stared at her hard for a long moment before again turning his back to her. While his hands played restlessly with the hat in his hands, he didn't turn back or say anything more, and finally she began to clear the table from their last dinner together.

"You're not bothering me here," he said at length, still staring at the hat.

"Mike…"

"No," he interrupted. "I…like having you here."

He turned to face her, attempting a smile, though it was far from the lighthearted expression he had intended. "You're a good cook. I haven't eaten so well in a long time."

"Thank you, Mike," she said. "That's really sweet of you to say, but I know what my being here is doing to you. I've disrupted your whole life, and you deserve better than that. Your home should be your castle, and it can't be that if my presence makes you too uncomfortable to even want to spend your time in it. You would rather be alone, and I should let you."

Again he turned away, playing absently with the hat in his hands, and again she turned her attention to placing the dirty dishes in the hot water she had waiting. She was halfway through with the washing up when he finally spoke again.

"I don't like being alone."

There was a deep loneliness in his tone now, as if the hardness had been a front he could no longer hold on to, and she stared at his back, trying to understand him, until he turned. When he saw her watching him he paced over to the window.

"Sometimes you just have no choice."

The desolation and depression in those words was heart-wrenching and Penny, feeling the desire to reach out to him, found herself moving closer until she was only a couple feet behind him.

"Mike, I owe you for saving my life," she said quietly as she stood there. "And I owe you for everything since. If there is anything I can do, anything at all…"

A strange, miserable laugh came from his throat as he turned on her.

"You don't know what you're asking," he said roughly.

"I do," she started as she took a step closer to him, but he moved away.

"No, you don't," he snapped. "You have no idea. You don't even know me. You don't know the first thing about me."

"I'd like to," she said. But that only seemed to increase his impatience with her.

"No, you wouldn't," he snapped even sharper than before. "You don't ever want to know me."

Reaching the door he turned back to face her. "You're right. You should go tomorrow – before you regret it for the rest of your life."

He then opened the door, tossed the hat on the table as a last-minute, deliberate thought, and walked out, closing the door behind him with a bang.

"Fool!" he called her in his thoughts as he walked away from the cabin. Blinded by the fact that he'd saved her life, she wasn't seeing what he was. She was trusting a man who was untrustworthy, she was admiring a man who would only disgust her if she was thinking clearly.

But, no, if there was a fool it was he. She didn't know the truth of him – what he had done, the shame he had brought on himself. If she knew she would feel as she should. She would know that saving her life could never repay for the sins of his past.

He should tell her. He should warn her before it was too late, before she was hurt irreparably, before things got out of control, before either of them made a mistake they would forever regret.

And yet it felt so good to be trusted again, to be cared about, even if he did not deserve it. And she had given him a gift. Simple though it was, she had made it with her own hands just for him. It spoke of her concern for him. It spoke of her wish to please him, of her trust in him and her gratitude toward him.

For so long he had known none of those things. No other person had cared for him or believed in him. No one had done anything special just to please him, to make him more comfortable.

And with reason. He was nothing. He was nobody. Diane had known that. But she had learned it too late to save herself. He couldn't let that happen to Penny. But neither could he bring himself to tell her the truth, to face the disgust he would see in her face.

She was right. It was time for her to leave. In her mind she would be leaving to make things easier for him, to repay his kindness by leaving him alone as she thought she wanted. And that was what he wanted, because alone he could go back to forgetting the past. And in forgetting the past he could forget the pain, the humiliation, the shame of who he was and what he had done to the woman he had once vowed to love for the rest of his life.

Yet, in reality, he knew her going would serve an even greater purpose. Her going would protect her from him. She would leave knowing only the heroics she saw in him after saving her life. She would not know the truth, and she would be happier for not knowing.

And when she was gone, still believing as she would in the good in him, maybe he could know a measure of peace. Knowing that just one person in the world believed in him – deservedly or not – could give him strength in the long, lonely years that would be the rest of his life.

Before she left, though, there were some things he did have to say to her. In order for her to protect herself upon her return he had to warn her about the woman who had attacked her and left her for dead. He also had to try to convince her to keep his existence a secret from those who would demand to know her story. And most importantly of all, he had to apologize to her for his harshness, to thank her for the gift of the hat that he would treasure for the rest of his life.

It was dark when he finally got control of his thoughts and returned to the cabin. Penny was already in bed and, though he knew she was still awake, she was still and silent as he came in. For a moment he hesitated to speak to her, uncertain now just what he wanted to say or how to say it.

First he checked the fire, but apparently she had just filled it, so he closed the stove and lay down on his rug, not even bothering to remove his shoes. After tonight he would be able to sleep in the bed again, he thought. But he found no thrill in that knowledge – knowing as he did that he would always see her there in his mind's eyes, and that such visions would make sleeping there harder than ever.

After entertaining the idea of waiting until morning to speak to her, he decided against it. She was awake now. She would feel more comfortable if he at least apologized, and so would he. So finally, still without fully knowing what he would say to her, he spoke up.

"Penny?"

"Yes?" Her voice was soft, uncertain, and he regretted having made her feel uncomfortable even for a minute.

"Thank you for the hat," he said for want of the right words to express his regrets.

Immediately she apologized. "I know it's not very good…"

"No, Penny, really, it's great," he assured her. "It's just…Penny, as you say, I'm used to being alone. I'm not used to people giving me things or…or fussing over me. I like the hat. And it will come in handy when the sun is hot."

She said nothing, probably uncertain what to say that wouldn't sound like fussing, and after a moment he sat up to remove his shoes and socks before lying down again to stare at the blackness of the ceiling lit only slightly by the quarter moon and the stars behind the trees outside the window."

"Before you leave tomorrow there is something you should know," he said after more than five minutes. As his thoughts turned and twisted restlessly he spoke them aloud, forgetting that she might be asleep by then.

Now, as the words cut through the darkness, he looked over to see if he had disturbed her sleep. As she didn't move or make a sound he couldn't be certain, but he felt certain she was still awake, so he continued.

"About what happened to you. I don't know how much you remember…"

It might be good to determine that first before he started making accusations against a woman he didn't even know who might have been a close friend or part of her family.

"I remember," she said quietly.

"You do?"

She sighed deeply and he knew she did remember. She remembered and, in remembering, felt deeply the betrayal.

"I remember," she said again in a faraway tone. He knew the pain. But he had never found a way to deal with it himself. He could not help her.

"I don't know who the woman was who hit you, but–"

"Caroline," she said. "Caroline Bower. We've been friends for eighteen years."

That was her pain. The betrayal of a friendship that had spanned such a large part of her life. Maybe that was even worse than the betrayal of a marriage vow that had only been spoken two years before. And he had deserved Diane's betrayal. Could Penny ever have deserved such treatment? He couldn't know it for a fact, but he found it impossible to believe it of her.

"Why did she do that?" he asked his question aloud.

"I don't know," Penny confessed. "I know she's…unpredictable at times, and sometimes she does things on the spur of the moment without any apparent reason, but she planned this."

She sighed again – confused and hurting, and he regretted he could offer her no consolation.

"You will be careful when you go back," he cautioned. "If she tried to kill you once–"

"I'll be careful," she promised.

Again they were both silent. The seriousness of Penny's situation was not lost on either of them, and Mike felt it as strongly as she did.

"Mike?"

Penny was the one to break the silence this time. "Thank you for caring. But I won't let her catch me off guard again. I'll…I will be okay."

"You will," he agreed.

"I will," she affirmed, more to herself than to him. "Goodnight."

"Goodnight," he acknowledged. Then, as an afterthought, added, "Penny? One more thing."

"Yes?"

"I would like to be left alone," he said. "You won't…tell anyone about me, will you? I don't want…reporters or…or grateful friends and family or anyone…bothering me – making a hero out of me or anything just because I happened to…find you out there."

He fretted as he waited for her answer which was several seconds in coming.

"I won't tell anyone," she promised finally. Though she spoke with reluctance he felt her promise would never be broken. Quietly she added, "But you are a hero." Then she turned over onto her side, her face to the wall, and shortly thereafter her even breathing told him she was asleep.

With the morning came rain by the buckets full. But it was the wind that first woke Penny before the sun was even up, whistling around the cabin with a fury that drove the rain into the side of the building. She was unaware how long she lay there listening to the wind and the rain, knowing it necessitated a change in her plans to leave today, yet seeing it as a sign that maybe she should stay a little longer. Her leg was far from healed yet, and while she felt sure she could make the trip if she had to, albeit very slowly, she was glad of the reprieve even of just one day.

Deep down she knew there was more to her wanting to stay than just concern about her broken leg. There was also concern for Mike. As she thought about him, and about his reaction both to her gift and to her suggestion that she leave, she realized it was not good for him to be so completely isolated, whether it was what he wished to do or not.

His claims of wanting to be left alone may have sounded sincere enough on the surface, but with deeper consideration she knew they did not ring true. The more she thought about it, with the wind and the rain howling outside, the more she was certain that his wanting to be alone was not as heartfelt as he made claim.

A loner, a hermit, a recluse – such a man must hate people, must hate the whole world, to want to escape it so carefully, so completely. And yet Mike had been kind to her. He didn't talk much. When he did speak to her it was with a reserve that seemed to agree with his claims of wanting to be left alone. And yet there was a loneliness about him that flooded his eyes at times, a vulnerability that cried out to be touched by someone – anyone.

And he had brought her flowers. Not only had he rescued her, bringing her to his secluded sanctuary to save her life, caring for her gently, tenderly, sympathetically. But he had brought her flowers. That one singular act of kindness touched her more each time she thought about it. If she hadn't been so out of it for so long she would have realized long ago that just that one act of kindness proved he had compassion in his heart. He had cared about her. He had wanted to make her, a complete stranger, feel better. No confirmed recluse would even have thought of such a thing.

And he had held her after her dream. That, too, was the act of a kind, compassionate man caring for the sufferings of another soul, the tenderness of a father with his child, not that of a man who hated the world so much he would choose to leave it behind forever.

And yet that was apparently what he had done. For some reason he had chosen to isolate himself completely from everyone and everything in the world outside this forest, and she felt certain it was due to the fact that, in some way she didn't understand, either the system or, more likely, some person he had loved had hurt him deeply.

It was only now that she was focusing so intently on him that she saw the pain, the hurt that ran deep through his soul. Until now her only thoughts about him were gratitude for his saving her and a desire to please him in return. But now she began to see him for the person he was behind the hero she had been seeing. He was still her hero, he always would be one after saving her life, but now she saw that he was human as well – sad, lonely, human. And for the first time she knew questions that desperately needed answers about this heroic benefactor of hers.

Not wanting to disturb him, she remained still in her bed until his stirring told her he was awake. It was only as he sat up to put on his shoes that she got out of bed to begin her day as well.

"It looks like you're going to have to wait a while to go," he said as he got to his feet to fold his blanket and place it on the end of the bed as it had become his habit to do.

"You think so?" she asked, though she had already come to that conclusion herself long ago.

"Maybe tomorrow," he said.

Penny said nothing as they began their morning ritual. Mike ran his comb through his hair, then loaned it to Penny to use as he shaved with the straight razor, going by feel rather than sight to be sure he was getting it done properly as they had no mirror.

While Penny prepared breakfast Mike took care of the fire, added water from the bucket to the pan on the stove, and brought up from the cellar the food she would use for the day so that she didn't have to climb down after it with her bad leg.

The chores and their meal were finished as usual in almost total silence. But, while Penny prepared to wash up the breakfast dishes and Mike made his usual beeline for the door to care for his outdoor chores, she felt the need to speak up.

"You can't seriously be planning to work out there in this?" she asked. If anything it was raining harder now than it had been when she'd first awakened.

Being the first time she had ever used that tone with him, or tried in anyway to tell him what to do, he was naturally surprised, but the stern, determined look he gave her made him look more vulnerable than angry, and it was ages that he just stood there staring at her while she hoped he would see sense. Apparently he didn't.

"I have to check the traps and bring in water and wood," he said, and he disappeared into the rain before she could protest further.

The man was a stubborn fool, she thought as she watched him through the window, walking away toward his trap line. Surely those tasks could wait until the storm abated a little. What difference did it make if he checked the traps now or this afternoon? It was only his foolish desire to stay away from her that prompted him to be so bullheaded. And for the first time she didn't feel sympathetic toward him, but instead felt impatient.

If he wanted to go out there and catch pneumonia that was his business, not hers, she fumed. He wasn't about to let her stop him from doing anything he wanted anyway, and she had no intention of worrying about him.

But she did worry about him. All the time she was washing the dishes she thought about him out there in the weather. He would, of course, be okay. He was tough. He knew his way around, and he had likely seen worse than this since he'd been living here. In fact, except for the fact that he would be drenched to the skin, there was really no danger to him out there at all.

It was only knowing her presence was the force that had driven him out there that upset her. If she had not been here he would have had no reason not to wait, and it bothered her that he preferred drowning out there in the rain over enduring her company. As she thought about it, and fumed over his stubbornness, she came up with a plan to reduce his excuses. She would just see what he did then.

Normally it took him an hour or more to walk his trap line. That gave her plenty of time to finish his other chores for him. When he returned he would be out of excuses for being out in the storm, and if he could spend all that time out in the weather surely he couldn't complain when she did the same, even if it meant taking over his work for him.

Her first task, barefoot as usual since she had no shoes, was to carry both water buckets out to fill at the spring. Mike always took both of them at once so Penny, after emptying the last of the water from the last bucket into the basin, hobbled out into the rain with a bucket in each hand.

By the time she had both buckets full, however, she discovered that they were too heavy for her to carry the way he did. After only a couple short steps she knew her leg would never hold up under all that weight. Even carrying one full bucket at a time made it difficult not to put too much weight on her bad leg and it was certainly feeling the strain. But halfway back to the cabin she found a nice stick to use as a walking cane, and that helped ease much of the strain.

After returning for the other bucket and getting both of them safely into the cabin, she made use of the outhouse before turning her attention to the firewood. Mike had a nice sized pile of it cut to length with his handsaw, but none of it was chopped to size for the stove. Penny was not about to let that stop her though. As drenched as she was she knew Mike was just as bad off, and she was determined that he would not have these tasks as excuse when he returned from the traps whether he liked it or not.

While Penny was chopping the short lengths of wood into stove-sized pieces with Mike's ax, he was checking his last trap. Possibly it was the weather that had kept the animals seeking shelter rather than finding his traps, but he found every last one of them empty and he felt frustrated at more than just the lack of meat for his dinner. The trip had been a complete waste of time and, after Penny's suggestion that he not go out in this rain, he anticipated her mocking his futility.

She would laugh at his stupidity in getting half-drowned without having anything to show for his efforts, and he would deserve every taunting insult. Thus, when he returned to the cabin to find her outside in the rain, as dripping wet as he was, hobbling toward the door with a small load of firewood in her arms he was stunned.

"What do you think you're doing?"

Because the noise of the wind and the rain had prevented her from noticing his approach until he spoke, his words startled her. But she hesitated only for a second.

"Helping," she said. "If the work has to be done in this weather than it is only fair that I help you with it so you don't have to be out here any longer than necessary."

Not waiting for his reply, she pushed the slightly ajar door open with her shoulder and carried her load inside. With a sigh he loaded the rest of what she had chopped into his own arms – three or four times what she was carrying – and followed her inside.

"That was a stupid thing to do," he said as he dropped his load on top of the three small loads she had already deposited in the wood box. "Look at you."

Penny didn't bother looking. She knew what she must look like – soaked to the skin, water dripping down her face and arms and legs in a steady stream, her hair hanging in long soggy strands over the shirt that was now plastered to her body. She knew what she looked like, because she could see it in him.

"Look at you," she said. "I'm no wetter than you are."

With impatience he moved over to the shirt hanging on it's nail by the stove.

"As we are now both soaked to the skin, who do you propose gets our one dry shirt?" he asked, holding it up to her as if to confront her with the unpleasant reality of their shared wardrobe.

Immediately he saw the regret in her eyes, the apology.

"I'm sorry," she said. "I didn't think about that."

"Obviously," he said. Abruptly he turned from the look in her eyes to toss the dry shirt over the back of the chair nearest him while he dried his face with the rag that hung next to his shirt.

"I'm sorry, Mike," she said behind him. "Naturally you should take the dry shirt. It's yours. I'll just stay by the fire until I'm dry."

He made no comment, just continued drying himself off with his rag as best as he could, rubbing the rag through his hair to keep the water from running freely down the face he'd just dried. Frustration at her carelessness in getting herself as drenched as he was when they had only one spare shirt between them was only part of his problem. More serious were the crazy feelings coursing through him as he contemplated the motives for her actions.

"You thought I was a fool for going out in the rain," he said without looking at her as he removed his wet shirt. "Just what kind of fool are you?"

Penny's instincts made her straighten up tall and proud behind him, her eyes glaring at his back, hurt by his accusation.

"I did not say you were a fool," she denied in a voice that reflected her hurt pride. "And I was only trying to help. You said the work had to be done. I figured if I helped you wouldn't have to be out there so long. But I guess I must be a fool if I thought you would appreciate that."

Turning her back to him, she stood facing the stove, only inches from the source of the heat that was going to have to dry her out. Tears of frustration and humiliation stung her eyes, but she refused to let them fall. Crying would only make her feel worse when he mocked her for them as well.

"Here, get out of that shirt and put this on," he said, handing her the dry shirt. "I'll keep my back turned."

"I told you, it's your shirt…," she started without even turning to face him.

But he insisted. "You can't stay in wet clothes," he said. "You'll catch pneumonia."

"Well, neither can you," she insisted impatiently. "And as you so rightly pointed out, it's my fault–"

He tossed the shirt at her, letting it land on top of her still wet head as she wouldn't take it from him, and instinct made her grab it into her hands as she turned finally to face him.

"I have jeans," he said. "You have nothing. Now are you going to change, or do I have to do it for you?"

She glared at him. Not once in all their time together had he spoken to her in this way. Normally if he wasn't avoiding conversation with her completely he was either speaking to her with kindness and patience or, more likely, an abrupt emotional distance. It infuriated her that he would insist on being so forceful, even angry now.

He had been impatient, even angry, with her before, but rather than being forceful about it he had just walked out. Now suddenly he was standing there threatening her if she didn't do exactly as he ordered.

Suddenly she laughed. Her eyes softened and sparkled as she grinned at him.

"What is so funny?" he demanded, caught off guard by the sudden change in her.

"My dear Mike," she said. "If I didn't know better I'd swear you were actually beginning to like me."

"What?"

The accusation stunned him. He could only stare at the absurdity of her words.

"I just realized it," she said, as if the very thing that shocked him amused her. "But this is the first time you have felt comfortable enough around me to let yourself go, to let me have a piece of your mind when I deserve it. I think I like that. This storm keeps up and we might actually get to be friends. Now turn around while I obey my orders."

Without waiting for his compliance she immediately began unbuttoning the wet shirt she was wearing. Before she had gotten the first button undone he had turned his back, and he stayed that way, stupefied and stunned by her words. Friends?! Yes, he could almost see her as a friend – even more than a friend.

And yet he dared not let himself do so. Friendship meant establishing an emotional bond that would only tear out his heart when she left him for her own world as he knew she would have to do eventually. It was going to be hard enough to see her go as it was, impossible to forget the sight of her lying on his bed, the feel of her clinging to him after her nightmare, the very smell of her long, silky hair–

"All done," she said as she hung the wet shirt by the fire to dry. "Your turn. I promise not to peek."

She sounded as if she was teasing, but it was impossible to find fault with the musical tone of her voice. It was not mocking, not as it would be if she knew–

Her face was toward the wall and he knew he'd better hurry up with his changing before she did start mocking him for daydreaming.

"You'd better wear some socks," he said as he finished dressing and moved to hang his wet clothes by the fire. "Keep your feet warm so you don't go getting sick on me. And those splints are wet. We'd better change them, too."

Now that he was clad only in socks and jeans, Penny had her first view of the solid wall that was his chest, and the firm strength of his biceps. It was enough to steal her breath away, but the fact that he was now back to that kind but impersonal tone of the past was enough to keep her focused on reality so that she didn't make a fool of herself staring at him. Regret that she had said anything about their being friends in the light of his reaction to that was enough, she didn't need to add to his discomfort by letting him see just how attractive she found him. She would really scare him off with that.

"I think you're right," she said. "My feet are a bit cold. What about you? Are you warming up enough without your shirt?"

Drat! She hadn't been going to say anything that would bring attention to his bare chest.

His grunted reply was indistinct as he got the first splints they had used before she had gone swimming in the spring. Without a word he indicated she sit on the bed where she could prop her leg up while he replaced the wet ones with dry ones with frowning concentration, as if he was adding fuel to the fire or some other mundane, impersonal chore. Penny chose to ignore his less than companionable attitude as she kept her eyes focused on his face.

"You're right," she said. "It was stupid of me to go out there like that. I'm sorry."

This time he didn't even grunt a reply, just gave a bare shrug with one shoulder as he wrapped the dry rags around the splints on either side of her leg and tied them tight. He was not cooperating at all with her attempts at conversation, but she was determined to get through to him one way or another, though it was clearly going to take some thought to figure out how to go about that.

When the splint was finished he placed the wet sticks and rags by the fire, wordlessly tossing her a dry pair of socks while he was at it.

"Tell me," she said as she slipped one sock over her foot, rolling it up below the splints rather than trying to stretch it out over them. "Who taught you this fine art of conversation you're dazzling me with here?"

Having decided she was being sarcastic he just gave her a very brief dirty look before opening the stove to add a piece of wood, even though it really didn't need it.

"You certainly do have a way with words," she continued undaunted. "You should write speeches for presidents and senators."

He kept his back to her so she couldn't read his expression, but she didn't let that concern her as she continued.

"But maybe you have been writing their speeches. Maybe that's why you're out here now. The speeches were so long winded even the politicians making them were bored."

Still he kept his back to her as he stood just staring down at the stove. And still she pushed.

"Of course it is possible you were the one making the long-winded speeches and the politicians ran you out of town so they would have a chance to get a word in. If you would only stop talking so much."

The fact that he still made no comment was frustrating. But he hadn't told her to shut up yet either, and she decided that was a good sign. She pushed still further.

"Maybe it was your barber who taught you to talk so much," she said. "He certainly didn't do any hair cutting. Maybe he was too busy talking to cut. Or maybe you were talking so much he–"

"Are you trying to pick a fight?" he asked, turning suddenly to face her.

His face was stern, but his eyes held no animosity. In fact, to Penny it appeared that he was amused and was trying desperately not to show it. It made her even bolder.

"Yes, I am," she said. "We have no more dry clothes to risk spending our time anywhere but right here in this cabin, but we are not going to sit in here all day staring at each other like two complete idiots. If that means fighting, then so be it."

His eyes held her own for a moment before he moved deliberately past her to a small drawer in a tiny cabinet at the foot of the bed. For one panicky moment she had visions of him taking some sinister method of avoiding this confrontation. But when he turned back around to face her he held a deck of cards in his hand.

"How about a game of Gin instead of a fight," he suggested. And there was actually a hint of a smile on his face.

"Sounds like a plan," she agreed with a smile of relief. "Though a fight might have been fun, too," she added with a grin as she followed him to the table.

"Another time perhaps," he said. And he actually smiled when he thought she couldn't see it.

They spent the morning playing cards, starting with Gin Rummy, which Mike won four out of five times. Penny didn't mind losing, though, because for the first time they were enjoying real conversation.

It was stilted at first. Mike had little to say, but it wasn't long before Penny managed to find a topic he felt comfortable with, and as they talked he began to relax, to feel at ease in their togetherness.

The subject that got them started was the cards themselves. Penny noticed their unique design as he was removing them from their box and she commented that she'd never seen any like them before. When his only comment was a faint shrug she asked, "Where did you get them?"

"They came with the cabin."

"No kidding. They must be really old."

He gave her a tolerant smile. "And why must they be old just because they came with the cabin?"

"Oh, I didn't mean the two necessarily went together," she said. "They just look old – antique."

He held up the deck to survey it carefully. "I don't know, they look to be in rather good condition to me."

"I meant the design," she said. "It's got an antique look to it, though if they are old they certainly haven't been used much. Are you sure we should be using them? They could be worth money."

"We either use the cards or we sit here staring at each other," he said. "Because I have no intention of fighting."

Her laugh was delightfully spontaneous. "Yes, sir, cards it is. Gin, did you say? I'm afraid you're going to have to remind me how to play. It's been a long time."

"I have a chance of winning, then, do I?" he asked, and she was pleased to see that he was teasing her.

"Don't be too confident, my friend," she said. "I do learn quickly."

"We'll see," was all he said.

As they played they talked, though not steadily, and Penny did most of it in the beginning. But as the morning wore on the conversation grew more and more comfortable until they really were like two old friends. The only complaint Penny had at all was that he wouldn't talk about himself. He did admit to having lived in the cabin for a year, and he was willing to talk some about the things he'd done to get settled in there, but he carefully changed the subject any time it got near anything else on a personal basis, especially his reasons for coming to the cabin in the first place.

Not wanting to ruin the growing peace between them, Penny didn't push him to reveal anything he wasn't ready to reveal, and when he turned the conversation to her own life she was careful to be as candid as possible. If she was open in discussing her own life with him maybe he would feel more comfortable sharing his with her.

So she told him about growing up with two brothers – one older, David, who was her father's accountant, and one younger, Peter, who was in college – and two younger sisters, Becky and Susie who were still in high school. She told him about the many family vacations in their own cabin in the woods, and the occasional weekend fishing trip. She talked of her parents and grandparents, her aunts and uncles and cousins.

"They must all be worried about you," he suggested seriously.

"Yes, they would be," she agreed, and for a moment the concern she felt for her worried family caused a frown to fill her face.

"The weather should be better tomorrow," he said. "We can get you back to them then."

His eyes were on the cards in his hands as he spoke. But in her own concern for her family, wondering what they must be thinking after her disappearance for so long, she didn't notice their sudden seriousness.

As if sensing her concerns, Mike was careful to direct the conversation to less emotional subjects for a while – spring in the Ozarks, her carvings and art in general. While they prepared and ate lunch together they discussed food and his garden, then again discussed cards after lunch as he taught her to play Casino. Still later, as the rain didn't let up, she taught him the game of Spite-and-Malice.

Despite the earliness of the evening, the storm made it too dark inside the cabin to enjoy playing cards any more, even with one of their rare candles burning, so after dinner, as thunder and lightening joined the wind and rain, Mike got her talking of other things to keep her mind off the electrical storm. As before, it was about nothing important. Mostly he just had her reminiscing about her childhood, but it was therapeutically effective in getting to forget her fears of the storm. It was only after the worst of it was over and Mike suggested that they blow out the candle and get some sleep that she realized what he had done.

"Thank you," she said as she snuggled down under her blanket. It looks like I owe you again."

"For what?" he asked innocently from his bed on the floor.

But she knew it had been deliberate, and she wasn't about to forget it.

"Mike, I know I get pretty crazy when the thunder starts rolling," she insisted. "And I know you only kept me talking to keep me from doing so now. So thank you for that. Goodnight."

Mike said nothing as he extinguished the candle, but she hadn't really expected him to comment and, as it was getting late, she turned on her side and was soon asleep. But it took Mike longer to fall asleep as his thoughts were filled with her. It was a long time since he'd spent a day like this one, relaxed, just playing cards and talking. But it was one he would not soon forget – even when she was gone forever from his life and memories were all he had left.

Chapter Five

With the passing of the storm the fog moved in, and by morning it was difficult to see the outhouse from the window. It wasn't especially cold, but a trip through the woods in that fog would have been a difficult task. It would be too easy to get lost in unfamiliar territory, so, when Mike suggested she wait for the fog to lift, she was only too happy to agree.

Mike, however, insisted on doing his outdoor chores, saying he knew his way through his trap line blindfolded so a little fog was not a problem, and he wasn't about to eat another meatless dinner. He did, however, insist she stay inside while he was gone. It was still very wet out there, and he didn't want a repeat of yesterday.

Because he smiled as he said that, she was only too happy to do as she was told, and he seemed pleased by her cheerful promise to obey. Now that he was more relaxed toward her she was also more relaxed. And she had at least one more day here with him. By the time she did leave maybe they could really be friends – friends enough that he would allow her to return for a visit once in a while.

After doing her own self-appointed chores – washing the dishes and cleaning the cabin as much as possible, she looked around for something more to do while she awaited his return. She could do some more carving, but she could think of nothing else to make, and anything she did start would likely only be half-finished if she was to leave tomorrow.

Since nearly the beginning of the conscious part of her stay she had been collecting animal skins – rabbits, squirrel, one possum – with the idea of sewing them together into some sort of garment. She had enough now to at least get started on that, but again, if she was leaving tomorrow she would have only just begun the project before she left, and that seemed a waste of time.

A game of solitaire would be a way of passing the time, she decided, and now she knew where the cards were. They were back in the drawer where Mike had found them yesterday. Kneeling before the small chest, she opened the drawer to find the box right on top of everything else. But, as she lifted the box out of the drawer, her eyes caught sight of something else – newspaper clippings poking out from under some other old papers and small books.

Thinking the clippings must be as old as the cards, curiosity about the story they might tell prompted her to pull them out for a look. Rather than being cut from the paper, they had been torn, leaving rough edges on all sides. Nor were they old, for the top one had a photograph she easily recognized as being Mike. Instantly the cards were forgotten as she laid them aside to take the clipping and draw it out into the light where she could see it better.

"*Convicted murderer, Michael Klotski, still at large,*" read the caption underneath a police photo of Mike.

"Convicted murderer." The words seemed unreal. Mike? It wasn't possible. And yet there he was in black and white, the newspaper photo looking like a wanted poster, complete with prisoner number.

"*Murderer Escapes Custody,*" was the title of the article in big bold print. She read the rest in a state of dazed disbelief.

"*Only twenty-four hours after being convicted of the shooting death of his estranged wife, Diane O'Claire – internationally acclaimed model – local businessman, Michael Klotski, has escaped police custody and remains at large.*

"*Klotski, one of three prisoners being transferred by prison bus to more permanent facilities where they were due to serve out their terms, was released when friends of another prisoner, Arnold Stone – convicted of armed robbery – ambushed the bus, freeing all three prisoners, wounding the driver and killing one guard.*

"Stone and his confederates were captured within an hour. The other prisoner, Jose Garcia, was returned to custody late last night while entering a friend's house. Klotski remains at large. Police ask that anyone seeing him use extreme caution in approaching him, and immediately call their local police station."

That was all there was to the short article, but it was enough to give her answers to so many questions that had plagued her for so long. It explained his coming out to the lonely seclusion of the cabin, staying here even when she knew he needed people. It explained the pain and the loneliness in his eyes.

But there was more, another article, also torn from the paper, also with a picture, lay underneath the first, and she quickly picked it up to learn all she could.

"Local Businessman Convicted of Slaying Estranged Wife," read the heading. The caption under a picture of Mike being led into the police station in handcuffs added, *"Klotski, arrested last April for the shooting death of wife, Diane O'Claire, was convicted of her murder in Judge George Lincoln's court yesterday."*

The article continued, "Michael Klotski, owner and founder of the Sunshine Health and Fitness Club, was convicted yesterday of the shooting death of his estranged wife, international model, Diane O'Claire. Though Klotski has professed innocence throughout his trial, prosecutors managed to convince a jury of his peers that he did in fact plan the cold-blooded murder of his wife after she left him for another man.

"According to witnesses, Klotski and O'Claire, married just under two years, were recently estranged after O'Clair revealed to him she was pregnant with another man's child. Klotski and O'Claire were overheard by neighbors as they fought over her affair. O'Claire was heard verbally abusing

her husband and, according to prosecutors, her taunts and condemnations enraged Klotski to the point of planned revenge. Three days after their altercation Klotski was found standing over the dead body of his wife, his own gun found at his feet, only minutes after neighbors heard shots fired.

"His wife's infidelity and subsequent departure gave him motive. The murder weapon, containing no fingerprints, was in his possession, and he was seen standing over her body only minutes after her death, giving him opportunity. With only his word to substantiate his claims of innocence the jury took very little time in reaching a guilty verdict. Klotski has been sentenced to twenty years in the state penitentiary. Friends of his were heard to say they were shocked that the man they had known and respected for so long could be guilty of such a horrendous crime."

For a long time after reading the articles Penny sat there just staring at them. She knew now the answers to so many questions. Mike was a man who craved freedom. That was why he spent so much of his time outdoors working, walking his trap line. Yet he had nearly lost that freedom for twenty years and only a chance occurrence had given him a reprieve.

It was not that he hated people or hated the world that had driven him into seclusion. It was knowing that if he went back, if even one person should recognize him and turn him in to the authorities, he would be forced to spend the next twenty years in prison. How deeply her very presence must have worried him. Just having her here must have–

The door opened, and she jumped with guilt as she turned to her right to face Mike, the clippings still in her hands. His eyes met hers – instantly aware of what she had discovered, and the look she saw there was a deep, agonizing pain.

"So now you know," he said.

It was as if her knowing his secret had sucked the life from him, and she felt an immediate sympathy for this kind man who had lost so very much.

"I won't tell anyone," she promised as she got to her feet.

He stared at her from the still open doorway for what seemed an eternity, his hand still on the knob where it had been as he'd opened the door. She had a feeling he was trying to determine her sincerity, and apparently he decided it was genuine.

"Then you're a fool," he said. And he turned and walked out, closing the door behind him.

Instantly Penny dropped the clippings back into the drawer and, without bothering to close it, hurried after him as fast as her bad leg would let her go, wrenching the door open just in time to see him walking off into the trees.

"Mike, wait!" she called, hobbling as quickly as she could after him.

He stopped, but he didn't turn around.

"I mean it, Mike," she said as she continued toward him, though slower now that he'd stopped. "I won't tell anyone about you. I won't say a word, I swear."

He turned slowly to face her. "You don't have to be afraid of me, Penny," he said. Deep pain filled his eyes, tearing at her heart as she stopped a few short feet from him. "I'm not going to…to shut you up or anything."

In an attempt to reassure him of her faith in him she gave him a smile. "I didn't think you were, Mike," she said quietly. "And I'm not afraid of you."

"Well you should be," he said harshly, turning his back to her. He would have walked away, but she wasn't about to let him go.

"I disagree," she insisted. "I see no reason in the world why I should be afraid…"

"Even though I'm a murderer?" he demanded, turning on her so abruptly that she jumped.

"Are you?" she asked.

His laugh was scoffing and self-pitying as he turned his eyes away for just an instant. "You saw the clippings. I was convicted by a jury of my peers."

"But you claimed you were innocent," she reminded him.

"Everyone claims they're innocent," he scoffed. "It's common defense procedure. It doesn't mean a thing."

"It does to me," she said. "If you tell me you didn't do it, I believe you."

He scoffed again. "Penny, you're..."

"Mike, I'm serious," she insisted. "You saved my life. I can't..."

"I saved your life," he agreed almost violently. "That doesn't mean you have to worship at my feet like some brainless idiot. Nor does it change the facts."

"Then tell me you did it," she dared him. "Tell me to my face that you took your gun and you sat in waiting to cold-bloodedly shoot your wife until she was dead. Tell me that to my face right now, and maybe—"

He looked as if he wanted to hit something in his frustration. "It doesn't matter if I did it or not," he yelled at her. "I was convicted. And your even knowing me makes you an accessory after the fact unless you turn me in. Is that what you want? Do you want to go to prison yourself for harboring a fugitive, a convicted murderer?"

"If that's what it takes," she said. "I will not send the man who saved my life back to prison, whatever anyone says, even you."

"Then you are a fool," he said.

"Maybe I am," she agreed. "Maybe I am the biggest fool who ever lived, and maybe I would feel differently if I actually thought you were guilty, But I don't believe that, and I won't—"

"I was convicted!" he shouted at her.

"And the prisons are full of innocent people convicted solely by circumstantial evidence. That doesn't mean–"

"I was found standing over Diane's lifeless body," he reminded her impatiently. "It was my gun. I had motive–"

"So tell me you did it," she dared again.

He turned vehemently, snapping off a small branch from the tree beside him in his hand. "Penny..."

"Mike, I'm serious," she insisted. "I don't think you did it, and I won't send you back to prison for something you didn't do."

"And what makes you so sure I'm innocent?" he asked, facing her again. "And don't say because I saved your life. That means nothing, even if you did know for a fact that it was true."

"I think your saving my life does mean something," she insisted.

"You were in no way responsible for what Caroline did to me. My even knowing about you puts your life and your freedom in danger. Yet you not only rescued me, but you brought me into your home. In order to help me you took the biggest chances you could have taken. And now that I know your secret you're willing to walk away from the only life you have rather than hurt me. You've been kind to me in every possible way – even bringing me flowers, and holding me after my nightmare. None of that is consistent in my mind with the personality of a man who could cold-bloodedly plan and execute another person's murder, and you're not going to convince me otherwise."

For a long time after her little speech Mike just stared at her, the pain and the turmoil in him mixed with a need to believe her trust in him. But such a belief was difficult for him, maybe impossible.

"You're a fool," he said again, this time in a whisper as he again turned away from her.

"Mike?!" she called after him as he walked away from her. But this time he didn't stop.

"You're the fool, Mike," she called to his back. "If you think shutting me out is going to make me go away, you are sadly mistaken."

Still he kept walking.

"You have a friend, Mike, whether you want one or not!"

But still he kept walking, and it was only as he disappeared from sight among the trees that she finally hobbled back into the cabin and closed the door.

As Mike walked off into the woods his thoughts tormented him more than they ever had before. When Diane had mocked him so blatantly the day she'd walked out on him he had hurt deeply, he'd felt betrayed and humiliated. But in reality he had known for a long time that things were over between them, he had just not allowed himself to believe that the fire was gone.

While they were still making love regularly, that was all they'd had left, and even that had lost much of it's spontaneity and feeling. It was more the act of fulfilling lustful desires than of expressing mutual love.

So, while his pride had hurt, her leaving had not really surprised him, nor had it really broken his heart. Her taunting had crushed his ego, and stomped his confidence into the dirt, but he had not been surprised by her going, only by the news that she'd had a lover for so long without his being aware of it.

By the time she'd called him on Monday, crying hysterically, even his pride was beginning to heal. If they were not in love, if Diane preferred Steve Duncan to her own husband, than maybe it was better for them both to be separated. Maybe, as she claimed, he was unworthy of her. After all, if he couldn't keep her happy, he didn't deserve her.

And then he had arrived at the house to meet her as she'd begged him to do, only to find her lying dead on the living room floor, covered in blood from the two bullet wounds, one that had apparently gone straight through her heart, the other penetrating deep into her brain. The shock of seeing her there had frozen him, the horror of seeing her lifeless body lying there in a pool of blood had prevented all rational thought for what seemed an eternity. He didn't even see the gun at his feet, he couldn't think what he should do.

Reason still had not returned as he finally knelt beside her, to touch the still warm flesh of the woman he had once loved. But there was no pulse, no breath filled her lungs, and he felt ill just being so near the blood and horror of death that she had become.

He could not think what had happened to her or why. He couldn't even fully comprehend that she was dead. And before he could do more than rise to his feet again, there were people facing him, accusing him of the horrible deed.

From that moment on the nightmares had not left him alone. People he knew and trusted, people he had thought of as his friends, doubted him. They were shocked and horrified that he had been caught red-handed, so they had not believed him.

Not that he blamed them. He knew how guilty he looked. He even felt guilty. Maybe he hadn't pulled the trigger, but what had he done to prevent it from happening, to protect the woman he had once vowed to love forever? He had done nothing. In fact, it was his own inadequacy as a husband that had driven her into the arms of another man. If not for his own repulsiveness as a man, she would not have had to go searching for affection elsewhere, and maybe then she would still be alive.

In an attempt to clear his name he, with the help of his attorney, had tried to learn what had really happened to Diane. As Steve Duncan appeared to be the only possible person other than himself with a motive, they had focused on him. He worked at the club, and thus had access to the gun Mike used for target practice on the club's practice range, and if Diane's call to her husband that morning was due to the fact she had changed her mind about being with him, it could have been a motive. He might even have framed Mike on purpose out of the same jealous rage.

But Steve Duncan's alibi had been airtight. He'd been at work, at the club, with at least a dozen witnesses to his whereabouts all through the morning. Unless he'd had help he couldn't have been involved, and they could find no leads on any other suspects to take his place. They couldn't even inject reasonable doubt into the minds of the jurors that it was a burglary or some other random attack that he had interrupted, because it was his gun, a gun that was kept at the club under lock and key.

Knowing the guilty party must have been someone he'd known well, someone with access to his gun, someone he had trusted – yet someone who hated him enough to deliberately frame him – had been a difficult concept to deal with, as difficult as the mocking taunts Diane had tormented him with only days earlier. Being doubted and condemned by all those he had thought of as friends had been just as devastating. Facing even a fraction of the twenty-year sentence behind bars that had been demanded of him, ostracized by society – everything had been a nightmare. And yet, none of it compared to the feelings that tormented him now.

For the first time since the nightmare had begun he knew a new pain. Whether he deserved it or not, Penny believed in him. Joe had stood by him throughout the trial. As his brother and only family he had been supportive and encouraging as no one else had. But even he had held doubts. But here was Penny – someone who had not even known him then – declaring avidly her belief in his innocence. And it was her very conviction that scared him to death.

As far as he could see there were only two possible reasons for her adamant defense of him. Either she was terrified that he would feel it necessary to kill her to protect his secret and was only proclaiming belief in him to protect herself. Or she really did believe in him. Neither possibility gave him comfort.

Naturally he would never take any steps to hurt her, even to keep her from telling the world what she knew of him, revealing his location. It meant moving on when she left, hoping no one would be able to pick up his back trail. But even if he should be caught he would rather spend those twenty years in prison without the chance of parole than ever to harm her in any way.

But the other possibility bothered him even more – the possibility that she really did believe in his innocence. Having Penny as an ally would be the greatest gift in the world, infinitely more than he deserved. But it presented incredible problems to which he had no answers, and the possibilities haunted him.

Did she really trust him as she claimed? If so it was only because he'd saved her life. So how was she going to feel when she was no longer with him day and night, when she had been returned to her own world where she belonged? Would she realize then that her belief in him had been only a fantasy?

Even if she stayed she would soon get over her hero worship of him once she'd gotten to know him better. She would see him then as Diane had known him to be – an inferior man with no redeemable qualities. Rough, basic, beneath contempt. Diane had learned the truth of him too late. Would it be too late for Penny as well?

But no. Even now she was probably regretting her stand in his defense – now that she'd had time to think clearly about all she'd read in those clippings. She would get it clear in her mind, and then she would think no differently than did the rest of the world.

And yet, he knew there was more to his pain even than that. Worst of all was his own feelings for the woman who had come – at death's door – into his life so suddenly. With every effort he had tried to distance himself for her emotionally. But that had turned out to be a fruitless endeavor. The harder he tried, the deeper his feelings ran, until he knew he was in love with her as he had never been with Diane.

From the beginning his relationship with Diane had been deeply charged. But it had always been founded almost completely on physical attraction and sexual pleasure rather than on real love. With Penny it was entirely different. Granted she was physically attractive, though in a more subtly charming way than Diane, but his feelings for her had nothing to do with her appearance.

They were based on her courage, her strength of character, her adaptability in dealing with all that she had been through – being attacked by a trusted friend, waking with a broken leg to find herself stranded in the middle of nowhere with a complete stranger, living under the basest of conditions without electricity or running water, a limited menu day after day, only his shirt for clothing and his surly company with which to share it all.

Diane would not have lasted one day in such surroundings, yet Penny had done so now for two weeks without complaining, with a smile, often humming little tunes throughout the day as she entertained herself and kept house for the two of them.

And she cared. In little things she was kind and generous, as well as industrious. If something needed done she did it – whether cooking and cleaning, killing her own dinner, carving her own dishes. Always she was doing little things to make life as comfortable for him as she could.

It was probably just her gratitude that prompted her kindness to him, though he knew she was instinctively a kind, generous person. Yet he would treasure her straw hat gift as long as he lived, whatever happened to him.

All of that made her unforgettable to his love-starved heart. He would always love her. He would never forget her gentle smile, her beautiful eyes. Long after she was gone he would see her lying in his bed, clad only in his shirt that reached nearly to her knees. He would feel her delicate body clinging to him as she sobbed in his arms. As long as he lived she would hold first place in his heart.

If it was in his power he would keep her with him forever. Yet he knew he had nothing to offer her. His home was a one-room shack in the mountains to which he didn't even have legal claim. He had nothing of value to offer her. He couldn't even offer her his love as he was a fugitive from justice and her only knowing him involved her in the dangers in which he had placed himself by running away.

Nor would the situation ever change. He would never be able to offer her more than he could at this moment, and for the first time since his escape he contemplated turning himself in. At least if he paid the price they asked of him maybe one day he would be able to get his life back.

But even then he knew he could never ask her to share it. It would be years before parole was a possibility, if they ever let him out after his being a fugitive for a year. He could not ask her to wait for him, even if she should be willing. She deserved better than that. From all she'd told him of her family and her life, he knew she came from a respectable family. She could not be asked to endure the ostracism and condemnation with which she would be faced for even befriending a convicted murderer – no matter how innocent he might be in reality.

And he was far from innocent. He had not pulled the trigger on the gun that had killed Diane. But neither had he been a man worthy of her love. Always he had been a crude man of uncultured and unpolished stature. His needs, his desires, had always been too simple, too basic, lacking sophistication and grace, breeding and refinement. No woman deserved to be saddled with a man so lowly and menial – especially a woman with Penny's kind spirit, her natural beauty and grace.

If it was in his power he would give her the moon as her pillow, the stars as jewels to frame her sweet face. And yet he knew she would never ask for such things. Even out here in the wilds of the untamed mountains she was content with only the little he had to offer her. Out here she was caught in a fantasy where he was a hero, where she believed in him, where she liked and trusted him, and he was loath to see her change.

But change she would, he knew that. In the real world, the world of love and respect from which he knew she came, where her family was waiting and worrying about her, he knew she would soon lose her hero-worship of him. As reality set in she would grow to hate him as she should, as Diane had done. Even if she should consent at this moment and time to let him love her, in the end he would only make her as miserable as he had made Diane. He could not do that to her.

Even without the conviction that hung over his head like an albatross, he was unworthy of her. With it he was a threat. If anyone ever discovered her association with him – even though she'd had no choice in the matter at all – she would be the one to pay the penalty. Even if she escaped conviction and punishment for befriending a fugitive, she would be condemned by her world as he had been by his.

No, never could he even let her know of his feelings. Never could he allow anything he had done, or anything he felt for her, to hurt her in any way. As soon as the weather cleared he had to take her out of here so she could return to her own world where she would soon forget him and get on with her life as she should. But as long as he lived he would never forget her. And the loneliness at the thought of losing her forever was almost more than he could bear.

The fog had been lifting steadily as he walked, and now it was gone, though a few higher clouds lingered giving the sky a dreary look. By morning the weather should be dry and clear, perfect for her journey out of these woods. She would go home where she belonged, but she would live always in the deepest recesses of his heart.

By the time he returned to the cabin it was well past their usual lunch hour, and he was starved. As he opened the door, though, the aroma of the stir-fried vegetables Penny had prepared told him she had waited lunch for him, and he knew a strong, empty longing as he realized this would be their last lunch together. One more dinner, one more breakfast, and she would be gone.

Cheerfully she jumped up from the table where she was sitting as he entered the room, and quickly she filled his plate and her own before returning to her seat. He stared with wonder at the items covering the table, which she merely pushed back enough to make room for his dish. He knew she'd been saving the animal pelts since she'd arrived, but now she had them all laid out on the table as if she intended creating something with them.

"What's all this?" he asked as he sat down in front of the plate she had served him.

She grinned. "Shirt making," she said. "Or coat making, or whatever it turns out to be when I get this all together."

"You're making clothes now?" he asked, amazed at this woman's talents. She may not win any prizes with her creations, but they did serve their purpose, all of them.

"Nothing that's going to win any awards for style," she said, cheerfully echoing his thoughts. "But then, who is going to see it out here?"

"Then why bother?" he asked. "You're leaving tomorrow."

"Not true, my friend," she denied with an impish grin. "I've decided to stay a while longer."

Chapter Six

Panic set firmly in Mike's heart as Penny declared her intent to stay. She couldn't be serious. How on earth could he cope with having her stay? It was going to be difficult enough to watch her walk out of his life now. And she would leave eventually. She had to. Even if she was grateful to him now, no woman could put up with this kind of life forever. But the longer she stayed before that happened, the harder it would be for him when that time finally did arrive.

"You can't be serious," he said aloud, hoping it was a joke.

"Oh, I'm very serious," she assured him easily. "I'm staying, so I'm creating clothes to wear while I do."

"But why?" he asked.

"Because you need me."

She spoke with a conviction that increased his nervous uncertainty. Panic guided his response.

"I thought you wanted to get back to your family. They're worried about you, remember?"

"Yes," she agreed seriously as she ate heartily of her lunch. "I will have to go back eventually, at least for a while, to let them know I'm okay."

"For a while?" It was only getting worse.

"You don't think I'm going to abandon you up here all by yourself when you need me so much, do you?"

"I don't need you here!"

Abruptly he got to his feet, irritated that she was making this all so difficult, yet terrified that she might learn just how right she was.

"I disagree," she said calmly. "But we can argue about that later–"

"I don't want you here!" he insisted, turning on her in his irritation, his agitation.

"We can discuss that later as well," she told him calmly, "though I don't believe it for a second. Right now, however, why don't you sit down and eat your lunch before it gets cold."

"I'm not hungry," he snapped at her. "And I thought you were in a hurry to go. You said it was time. You gave me reasons."

"So I did," she agreed, still so calm it was frightening. "But that was before I knew just how much you needed me."

"I don't need you!" he shouted at her. "I've done perfectly well without you for more than a year. I don't need you now. I can cook for myself, wash my own dishes–"

"Of course you can," she agreed. "But that's not what you need me for."

"I don't need you at all! I don't want you! I just want you to go away and leave me alone!"

"You want to know what I think?" she asked, still calm, irritatingly calm, as if this was not the most terrifying conversation they'd ever had.

And he didn't want to know. He was terrified to hear it for fear she was reading his very mind and heart, his soul, as no one ever had. But she only grinned cheerfully as he snapped out his claimed disinterest.

"Well, I'm going to tell you anyway," she said. "So why don't you sit down and have a listen. After that you can tell me what you think."

For a moment he just stood there glaring at her, knowing she was not about to give up, yet knowing equally well he didn't want to hear anything more than that she was ready to go. But finally he sat back down at the table and picked up his fork, concentrating on his meal rather than her irritating cheerfulness that frightened him so much.

"The other day I told you I thought it was time I left," she admitted, "and at the time I thought it was. You apparently wanted to be left alone and after all your kindness to me I thought it best to do as you wanted."

"Good thought," he grumbled without looking at her.

She smiled gently for just a moment, though he was staring at his food so he missed it. Then she grew serious.

"But even then I was concerned. You put on airs of wanting to be alone – a recluse, a hermit. But all the while you were being kind, gentle, understanding, generous... And there's a loneliness in your eyes that cries out for friendship."

"I don't need your pity," he said. His jaw set firm as he met her eyes with what was almost a threat.

"And I'm not offering any," she said seriously. "But knowing all that you've been through has helped me to understand you better. I see now that your pushing me away is not a desire to be left alone. It's a defense mechanism. You like me, you want me here, even if just so you don't have to be so alone..."

He would have protested, but she refused to give him the chance.

"...but you want to protect me form the stigma of association with you, and you want to protect yourself from being hurt again. All of that is completely understandable. But I don't think being so alone is good for you, and I'm not letting you push me away."

His jaw was clenched so tight it hurt. His eyes growing harder still as he pushed away the pain she had claimed to see there.

"I don't need a psychologist," he said in a tone that, while low, was harder than stone. "I don't need you analyzing me, telling me what you think I'm thinking–"

"I'm not trying to psychoanalyze you, Mike," she denied quietly. "I'm only trying to be your friend. You have done so much for me, everything lately. It's my turn to do something for you."

"Then leave," he said, rising again to his feet to walk to the stove, staring down at it with his back to her, wrestling violently with his own thoughts and emotions. The last thing he needed was her friendship. There was no future in it, and he wasn't ready for the emotional stress involved. But instinctively he knew she was not giving up so easily.

"I can't leave," she insisted in a quiet but firm voice.

He turned on her. "You're not helping me by staying," he argued vehemently. "I don't want you here. I don't need you–"

"I think you do."

He felt the need to hit something in his frustration, but she pretended not to notice.

"Mike, I've read the clippings. I know how hard it must have been for you. Your wife, the woman you loved, was unfaithful to you. That must have hurt like crazy—"

"So I killed her," he interjected, his back to her.

"I didn't say that," she denied. "I didn't even think that. I don't think it's in you to have purposely hurt her, never mind kill her."

"Then you don't know me as well as you think you do," he said, turning on her again. "When I'm angry—"

"But that's just the point," she insisted. "According to the newspaper accounts you didn't even touch her when she stood there telling you she was pregnant with another man's child, that she was leaving you to be with her lover. She wasn't killed for days after that. If uncontrolled anger was your motivation you would have struck out at her then. But you didn't – because it's not in you to do so."

"I was waiting my chance to do a thorough job of it," he said, apparently repeating the prosecutor's accusations.

"And I don't buy that," she said. "Let's say for the sake of argument you could plot a cold-blooded murder – which I don't believe for a second – you're no fool. You wouldn't have done it with your own gun, in your own house, loud enough to bring the neighbors running, and then stand over her body just waiting to be caught. You'd have to be a fool."

"I am a fool," he said, more to himself than to her, regret filling his eyes as he stared blindly into the past.

"You are not a fool," she denied. "You're just a man – a man who loved and trusted and was betrayed for your trouble. I understand that. I've been there. It hurts. It hurts worse than anything else ever has, and you think—"

"Robert," he said, remembering the name she had sobbed to him after her nightmare.

Surprise hit her. She remembered talking to him about her family, but she hadn't mentioned Robert, had she?

"You mentioned him the night of the storm," he said, seeing her confusion.

"Oh, yes, he was in my dream," she recalled. "We were engaged. But then he–"

"He what?" Mike asked, genuine compassion in his tone as she hesitated. "He betrayed you?"

She gave him a smile. "You're trying to change the subject."

"I think this is the subject," he insisted. "You want to psychoanalyze me. You want to delve into the deepest recesses of my soul whether I like it or not. Well, I contend that this delving is a two-way street. You want to psychoanalyze me I get to psychoanalyze you first."

Penny conceded with an amused smile. "Okay, My Friend," she said. "You want to hear about Robert. I'll tell you everything there is to tell. You can ask any questions you wish, and I will answer as completely and honestly as I can. But when I'm through, like it or not, it's your turn."

Immediately he regretted making that remark, but she was already speaking.

"So, Robert. We met at college. We dated some then, but not seriously until after graduation. I pursued the relationship. He was good-looking, charming, sense of humor, family money. The only thing that mattered to me, though, was that he was a lot of fun to be with. Our dates were always fun and exciting, and he respected my wishes to wait for our wedding night to consummate our relationship, so I thought nothing could be better. Most of the guys I knew were constantly pushing in that regard, but Dad has always made us kids feel if you really love a person with the deep, lasting kind of love that's going to make a successful marriage, than sex is not of primary importance. And if a man can't wait he doesn't really love you. So when Robert was willing to wait I figured it meant he must really love me."

She stopped to look at him, her expression clearly an expectation that he would mock her for her ideals, for her virginity, but he knew he felt no such thing. In fact, the knowledge that she was a virgin made him love her that much more. Slowly he returned to his seat across the table from her, giving him an excuse to avoid her eyes.

"Robert, however, was a spoiled, little rich kid without a backbone of his own," she continued when he said nothing. "His father told him what classes to take in college and what career he would pursue. His mother dressed him and planned his social life. He had everything he wanted the minute he wanted it and never had to even think for himself about what he wanted in life. Only I didn't know any of that until we were actually engaged."

As she talked about Robert, Mike watched her return to her animal-skin garment, poking holes in the edges with his knife, then poking long thin strips of the hide into the holes to sew the pieces together. It was slow, tedious work, but she did it absentmindedly as she talked.

"In all fairness to Robert, I suppose what happened was not entirely his fault," she continued. "His mother was determined to break things up between us from the minute she heard about our engagement. She even offered me fifty thousand dollars if I would call it off, and she was furious when I turned her down."

"You turned down fifty thousand dollars for this guy?" Somehow that thought filled him with a jealous pain. She must have loved the man deeply.

"Of course I turned it down," she said. "I was marrying Robert, not his family's money. Nor did the thought that Robert would be disinherited if he went through with it bother me. But apparently it bothered Robert. He was used to money. He didn't think he could live without it, so he called it off."

"I'm sorry," Mike said with compassion as she stopped and turned her eyes to his, apparently seeking some comfort from him.

"That wasn't the worst of it," she added. "Robert didn't have the guts to tell me to my face that he preferred his family's money to me. He preferred to have me break things off, and he figured the only way he could get me to do it was to let me catch him having an affair with another woman. He preferred to be seen as unfaithful than to be seen as mercenary."

"I'm sorry," Mike said again, knowing how hurt she must have been when she had given her heart to the man.

She gave him a smile. "Why?"

Instantly he grew cautious. "Why what?"

"Why are you sorry?"

"What?" He couldn't even comprehend her question, never mind answer it.

"Why are you sorry?" she repeated. "Why would you be sorry for me just because I was dumped for a fortune by the man I thought I would love forever?"

He didn't answer. He could only stare at her as if she'd lost her mind.

"I know why you're sorry," she continued when he couldn't seem to find his tongue. "You're sorry because you're a kind, caring person who hates to see another person suffer. And because you also have been hurt by the person you loved, you know how that feels. You can understand the pain involved, you can empathize with those feelings. So give me credit for the same understanding toward you."

This time he didn't argue. Even the look in his eyes changed as he saw her point. And he did need a friend so badly. Maybe–

"It was different for me," she admitted more quietly as he remained silent. "True I was hurt, devastated for a while to think that Robert hadn't loved me enough to even be honest with me, that money meant more to him than I did. But I had people to turn to, people who cared, people who listened, who loved me and helped me through that. And I was never faced with Robert's death or accused of his murder. I don't know what that would have been like – to go through all that pain and have even my friends doubt my innocence."

"I didn't say my friends doubted me," he said, avoiding her eyes as the pain of the memory came back afresh.

"I read the clippings, Mike," she reminded him. "Comments by your friends… Maybe they wanted to believe you, but there were some of them at least who didn't. So who did you have to turn to? Who did you have to believe in you? To stand by you through that nightmare?"

He said nothing. She knew. He knew she did. Maybe she didn't know about Joe, but even with his brother at his side, trying to believe in him, he had felt abandoned and alone. Never had anyone understood him as Penny seemed to now. But the concern she showed him was almost more than he could stand.

Putting her sewing work aside, which she had already stopped working on, she got to her feet to come and kneel beside his chair, looking up at him with compassion in her eyes. He couldn't make his eyes leave her face.

"All I want to do, Mike, is to help," she said in a quiet voice he couldn't ignore. "Talking to the people who cared about me is what helped me through that. And now I'm here for you – to listen to anything you have to say – as your friend. Anything you say to me will be solely between us. I will never betray your confidence. I hope you can believe that."

Looking down into the sincerity of her eyes he knew he trusted Penny with his life. She would not betray him or mock him as Diane had. She would take his word at face value without ever doubting him. She trusted him. She believed in him. It was the very thing his soul had craved for two years – since that day he'd stood before Diane's merciless taunts. And yet it terrified him.

"I won't push," she said after a minute. "Take your time. I'll be here when you're ready – for as long as you need me."

That would be a long time, he thought. As long as he lived he would need her at his side. But he had no right to ask such a thing of her and guilt and uncertainty made his ask, "What about your family?"

"I know they're worried," she admitted. "And I will have to go back soon to let them know I'm okay. But they'll be alright. They have each other, you have no one. Besides, I don't think my leg would hold up for a trip like that just now, and I can't risk exposing you by wearing your shirt back to civilization, so I need some other clothes to wear before I leave. But even then I won't go so long as you need me. Never while you need me, I promise."

"Penny–"

"I mean it, Mike," she insisted. "When you're ready to talk I'm here."

He stared at her long and hard for a long moment, then sighed as he accepted the inevitable.

"You are the pushiest person I've ever met," he accused with a nervous laugh.

She grinned. "Only when necessary."

"Well, it's necessary right now for me to make a little trip out back," he said as he got to his feet. "You'll have to excuse me."

He knew she could see clearly through his delaying tactic, but he just wasn't ready to confide in her. He'd been alone too long to adjust to her friendship, her trust and concern, so easily. But it did feel good to have her here. He only hoped when she was gone he would not go completely out of his mind with the loss of her.

"Do you mind if I ask you something?"

Night had fallen so Penny and Mike were, as usual, in their respective beds, but Mike had a lot on his mind, and he knew she was not yet asleep. He didn't even think about his need to talk, he just let it have it's way.

"Ask away," she told him.

"What was the name of the woman who…brought you out here?" he asked.

"Caroline," she said. "Caroline Bower."

"Caroline," he repeated absently. "So how did she and Robert get along?"

"Caroline and Robert? I don't know, they tolerated each other, I guess. Why?"

"They weren't friends?" he asked.

"Not friends," she agreed. "Robert thought she was a flake, and she saw him as a Mama's boy."

"How well did they know each other?"

Penny could see no reason for his interest in the relationship between Robert and Caroline, but wanting him to feel comfortable talking to her, she conceded to tell him anything he might want to know.

"We both met Robert in college," she said. "Caroline actually met him first. They even dated a time or two, but they didn't hit it off very well, so it didn't last."

"Who broke it off between them?" he asked.

"It was pretty mutual, I think," she said.

"How did she feel about you marrying him?"

Penny gave a little laugh as she thought about it. "She gave me a big speech about what life would be like married to a Mama's boy and suggested if I wanted to be that miserable I could just as easily jump into a pool of piranhas about their feeding time."

"She was pleased then when your engagement was canceled?"

"Well, Caroline is seldom especially elated by anything," she said. "But she did assure me I was better off without him. At the time, though, I was too involved in my own feelings to pay much attention to hers. Why? What are you thinking?"

"How long has it been since Robert called it off?" he asked rather than answering her question.

"I don't know," she said. "I've been here for how long?"

"A couple of weeks," he said.

"It was probably a week and a half before that on a Thursday."

"And you immediately told Caroline what happened?"

"Actually I didn't have to," she said. "She was one of the many people who saw him with the other woman. She came to me for an explanation. But by then I'd already talked to Robert and I was terribly depressed. I sobbed on her shoulder, confessed the whole thing, and she assured me I was well rid of him."

Mike was quiet then for several minutes as he thought over all that, and Penny pondered his reasons for asking. It wasn't just idle curiosity, of that she was sure.

"Mike?" she asked finally. "Why the questions? What are you thinking?"

"Just trying to understand why someone you saw as your friend would try to kill you," he said. "You really have no idea why she did that?"

"You would have to know Caroline to understand that," she said.

"Caroline is…well, a bit unbalanced at times, I think. She'll get the craziest ideas about things, or she will get these sudden urges to hit out at things. I've never known her to go to such extremes before, but there's always a reason somewhere inside her head that is perfectly logical to her for everything she does. She may have decided I had done something wrong and the urge just came over her to do something about it. She may not even have meant to hurt me."

"She meant it," he said. "I saw her. I was too far away to do anything about it in time, but I saw it. She had the weapon in her hand, she hit you with it, stripped you of your clothes, and very calmly pushed you over the edge of the cliff. If the brush hadn't cushioned your fall you would have been dead from that alone."

Penny shuddered. She knew that to be the truth. She knew Caroline had acted deliberately, and that she would at this moment be lying there dead if not for Mike. But hearing it put into words made it sound terribly ominous.

"I'm not trying to frighten you, Penny," he said. "But what she did was premeditated. And if she had reason to do so once she won't hesitate to do so again."

"I know," she said quietly. "I'll be careful."

"Careful may not be good enough, Penny," he insisted. "Whatever her reason, you've got to inform the authorities so she can't—"

"I will, Mike, I promise," she said. "The minute I get back I'll tell my father what happened. He will take care of it."

"I suppose you think I'm being unreasonable," he said. "That I'm butting in where I don't belong…"

She smiled into the darkness, her smile reflecting in her voice even though he could not see it. "No, of course not. I'm glad you care. But I will be okay, I promise."

Mike was silent for a moment before he asked. "You don't think her reasons had anything to do with Robert?"

"You mean like jealousy or something?" she asked. "I can't think why. Even if she was secretly in love with Robert we'd already broken up. And she wouldn't have wanted to punish me for breaking up with him. She didn't even like him. If anything she would have wanted revenge against Robert for hurting me. I see no reason at all that she would want to hurt me."

"Well, she did," he reminded her. "With premeditation."

"I know," she said. "But I won't give her another chance."

There was silence again in the darkness as Penny's thoughts turned from Robert and Caroline to Diane. Someone had possessed a powerful reason to want her dead as well. Someone who was willing to frame Mike in the process by using his gun and doing the shooting just as he was coming in the door so he would be found standing over her body.

"Who do you think killed Diane?" she asked aloud.

"Diane?" The question caught him off guard.

"You didn't kill her, so who did? Her…boyfriend?" She'd almost said lover, but had decided against it in case it was too strong a reminder of his wife's unfaithfulness.

"He had an airtight alibi."

"Oh," she said, aware from his tone that he'd thought of that already, had checked it out thoroughly in an attempt to defend himself. "Then who? Who else had motive?"

"Don't you think I haven't tried to figure that out?" he asked, his pain filling his tone.

"I'm sorry, Mike," she said. "I know you have. It's just that now I'm wondering too. If we're going to get you exonerated we're going to have to start somewhere."

"Stay out of it, Penny. Just leave it alone."

"I won't say anything to anyone to get you in trouble," she promised.

"You'll be getting yourself in trouble," he said. "Whoever killed her is safe now, but you go snooping and you'll stir up a hornet's nest. You could get yourself killed. And even if you don't, they'll wonder how you got involved with me, and they'll know you must have met up with me out here. They'll come looking for me, and they'll throw you in prison for harboring a fugitive."

"I won't say anything," she promised. "I won't snoop. I just thought if we talked about it maybe we could get some ideas."

"We wouldn't get any ideas," he insisted. "My attorney spent a year trying to come up with an idea, and he had the evidence in his lap. You know nothing about it."

"That's just the point," she argued. "I can start from scratch, a fresh view point–"

"And what good would that do?" he asked. "You couldn't do anything about it without getting me caught and sent back to prison, and getting yourself in just as much trouble."

"I won't do anything to get you sent back, I swear," she promised again. "But if we did come up with something I could make an anonymous call to your attorney or the police or something. They wouldn't even have to know it was me."

"You're a dreamer, Penny," he said.

"Maybe I am," she admitted. "But it can't hurt to try. And I promise I won't do anything you don't want me to do."

That was the last persuasive thing she said. If he wanted to confide in her he would, but pushing was not going to make him do anything he didn't want to do.

And then he did tell her his story. He started slow, intending only to tell her enough to make her see the fruitlessness of her desire to help him. But once he'd started talking the words just seemed to keep coming and coming. Two years of marriage, his wife's betrayal, her violent death and his own arrest, trial and conviction, his fears, his pain – everything came out there in the darkness as if the dam he'd held over his emotions for so long had at long last burst open with relief.

While she made the barest of comments along the way he told her about Diane's moods, how she had been so secretive about her daily activities while he was working at the health club he had founded years earlier. Occasionally Diane had dropped by the club to see him, which was where she had met Steve Duncan, but more often than not he didn't see her until he came home at night and she never talked about what she'd done all day.

A model of international fame, she'd had her own work to do much of the time. Despite a twinge of jealousy on his part that the whole world was in love with her, he had not wanted her to feel he was depriving her of her own career just because she was married to him. So he had tried to be supportive whenever possible. But gradually things grew less and less perfect between them.

If Mike called her at home during the day she was not there. If he asked her about her day she grew defensive and evasive. If he invited her to join him for lunch at the club she usually pleaded a headache or some other excuse not to meet him. If she did join him she was invariably late with no excuse at all for her tardiness.

Being a model he knew she had her own work to do, and usually when he had asked her about her day she'd informed him she wanted to forget work as long as possible, so he had not pried. He'd understood the need to keep business separate from their relationship, so he had never once suspected she was seeing another man. Even when he had felt the closeness of their relationship slipping away from him he had suspected only that the honeymoon had worn off, that they were finally settling into the routine that was married life – never had he suspected that she'd found the need to be with another man.

Thus, when she'd finally confessed her affair to him he had been both surprised and hurt. Never had he suspected she was dissatisfied with his affections or his attentions. Though they had drifted apart emotionally, their sex life had been fully as passionate and satisfying to him on the very night before she'd walked out on him as it had been the very first time – though he had to admit that that part of their relationship was quickly becoming all they had left between them – and he been certain it was equally satisfying to her.

He told Penny everything. He hadn't meant to. He'd intended only to satisfy her curiosity so that she would leave him alone. But once he was started he couldn't seem to stop until he had told her every detail. After telling her everything about his and Diane's relationship, about her mocking him with her adultery and walking out, he told her about her call that last morning, about finding her body and about his arrest. He told her of the trial, of his feelings of hopelessness, of being abandoned by everyone he had once thought of as his friends, how only Joe had stood by him, and even he had possessed doubts. He talked about being in jail, about awaiting the outcome of the trial, about the horrible blow it was to hear the sentence against him.

And then he told her about the escape. The whole experience was etched into his brain until it was a permanent fixture. He would never forget even a moment's detail, including the feelings – the fears and anxieties that had gone with the event – and he told Penny everything.

After the trial and the undeserved conviction he had been despondent and depressed. His own feelings of guilt at not being man enough to keep his wife happy added to his depression. If he had done his part maybe she wouldn't have gotten involved in whatever had gotten her killed.

At this point Penny said quietly, "You can't control another person, Mike. No matter who they are or how much you love them, their destiny is of their own making. And you said yourself she still responded to your love-making as she should. You couldn't have done more than you did."

"She obviously didn't think so," he said, unable to forget those taunts, or the pain of knowing she had been with another man because she had found him so inadequate.

"That's not necessarily true," Penny said. "There are people who are…well, addicted to sex or adoration and attention. In that case she would have taken all she could get from you and still wanted this Steve Duncan, maybe even others. There's nothing you could have done about that. It would have been her decision, her life. The only way you could have prevented her from taking such a course would have been to lock her up like some sort of concubine. And that's rather illegal in this country I think."

Mike was silent in the face of her attempted levity as he pondered her words. He wanted to believe them, but he'd lived with the guilt for so long it was difficult.

"So what happened?" Penny asked after a minute. "The bus you were on was hijacked?"

Grateful to be discussing his escape rather than Diane, he told her about his feelings of depression turning to fear as the bus suddenly swerved dangerously with a flat tire. Instantly five masked men armed with semi-automatic weapons descended on the bus, demanding the release of all the prisoners. It was the most terrifying moment he could ever remember facing as he sat there helplessly handcuffed to the bus with five crazy, angry armed men shouting and shooting around him, but in the end he had found himself released from custody.

"Go on, get out of here," they'd demanded, and he hadn't had to be told twice. Fearing for his life he'd raced off through the trees like the coward he was.

"There's nothing cowardly in avoiding a confrontation with five armed men," Penny assured him.

"I was a coward," he insisted. "I was scared to death, so I ran."

"And what could you have done if you'd stayed?" she asked. "Got yourself killed? That would have accomplished nothing. And you would have been a fool not to have been afraid."

Again he was silent for a while, but suddenly she heard him chuckle. She liked that sound.

"You're good for my ego," he said. "Anyway, once I stopped running long enough to think, I knew I couldn't go back, not voluntarily at any rate. I was free, and I intended to stay that way."

"So what did you do?" she asked. "How did you avoid getting caught?"

He told her. After running as if his life depended on it until he was ready to drop, he finally stopped to think, and he quickly realized several things. Most importantly he knew that without a plan he would be caught in no time at all. The authorities were probably already on his trail with bloodhounds or some sort of expensive equipment. He was just running without a goal, and he was sure he must have left them quite an easy trail to follow.

He was also aware that he had no place to go. The only person he might have counted on to help him was Joe, and the authorities were sure to be watching him already, as well as any place else they thought he might go. If he was even to contact anyone he knew they would catch him.

Only two possibilities faced him at that point so far as he could see. He could turn around, turn himself in, and spend the next several years incarcerated for a crime he hadn't committed, or he could run away forever from his life – from the brother who was his only family, from his business, from everyone and everything he knew.

It had been a hard choice. He hadn't wanted to go to prison, but neither had he wanted to be on the run for the rest of his life. So he had wrestled with his thoughts for a long time. But in the end he could see no reason for going back. Even if he served the time they asked of him he would have lost everything that mattered – most especially the respect of his friends and his customers.

And to be locked up day after day, year after year – he knew it would drive him insane. Even the time he'd already spent behind bars had affected him deeply. He couldn't bring himself to give in to that freely when the opportunity for freedom had been given him.

Then, while still in the middle of his warring thoughts, a heaven sent opportunity was dropped in his lap. As he sat under the trees contemplating his options, he heard the sound of a motor, and he realized he was only about twenty feet from a dirt road that twisted it's way through the woods.

His first instinctive thought was that it was the police searching for him and instantly he hid himself from sight. But it wasn't the police. It was a noisy, old pickup with a canopy on the back. The older couple inside seemed to be lost as they stopped only a dozen yards from him to inspect a map, apparently arguing over whose fault it was that they'd made a wrong turn.

As Mike stared at them from his hiding place an idea formed. He had no idea who they were or where they were going, he wasn't even sure where he was. But he did know that if he was going to avoid recapture by the police he had to get away from that place as quickly as possible. The old pickup seemed too great a coincidence to pass up.

The canopy had no door and, as their attention was on their map, suddenly he knew he had to take a chance. As quietly as he could he sneaked out of his hiding place toward the back of the pickup, careful to keep the brush between him and the pickup until he could safely reach the back without being seen.

Their attention never left the map as he, slowly so as not startle them with the sudden movement of the vehicle, stepped up onto the back bumper, raised his leg over the tailgate, and crawled under the canopy. Apparently they were on a vacation, possibly to visit their grandchildren, because the back of the pickup was filled with luggage and gift-wrapped packages. For fear they would stop and catch him back there he stayed low and out of sight, yet ready to jump and run in an instant at the first sign of trouble.

But there was no trouble. After a few minutes they started moving again. The pickup was turned around just a short distance up the road, and they went back in the direction from which they had come. Soon after that they were on a paved road, then on the highway for about five minutes before turning onto the road they had apparently been looking for in the first place.

For miles they drove on with Mike hiding in the back, not stopping until they reached Barstow, and pulled into the driveway of a family home. Fear that they would immediately come looking for their luggage had him alert and ready to make a run for it, but they didn't. Instead they went straight up to the house where they met a whole family of people who eagerly invited them in, and he made his escape as quickly and unobtrusively as possible.

He now found himself in the suburbs off Barstow with people everywhere. He had no money, no credit cards – nothing. And the clothes he wore, while not the striped prison garments he'd seen in the movies, were distinct enough that anyone taking a good look would instantly have been aware that he'd escaped from police custody. The police were certain to be looking for him by that time and, though he was many miles from the place where they had lost him, as well as from his home in Riverside, he knew that caution was of utmost importance.

Not daring to show his face until dark, he stayed hidden in an alley, cautious and alert every minute even while his hunger and discomfort grew rapidly. But escape was his first concern and personal comforts had to come second. Thus he kept to dark alleyways and unlit streets for more than an hour careful not to let anyone see him as he tried to figure a way out of the area without being seen. It was after midnight when he spotted a gas station near the freeway.

A pickup with an empty horse trailer on behind was parked in front of the pumps, the driver inside the building out of sight. Mike stood contemplating his chances in getting inside that trailer without being seen, but before he could make a move to try it, the driver exited the building, catching sight of him immediately, though apparently not recognizing him.

"Looking for a ride?" the man asked.

Not wanting to make the man suspicious, Mike had decided to take the ride offered and by morning he found himself in Los Angeles. That was the exact opposite of the direction he had been wanting to go, but he was afraid the man giving him the ride would get suspicious if he asked to get out too soon, so he spent that day hiding out in the city.

Desperately hungry by that time he was contemplating scrounging for food in garbage cans when he spotted a dollar bill on the ground. It was covered in dirt and grime, as if it had been run over a time or two, but it was enough to get him a hot dog to stave off starvation.

Later, as he continued to hide out until dark he came across a pile of used newspapers awaiting the recycler. From them he obtained the articles Penny had read. It was then that he knew he had to get as far away from California as he possibly could. With his picture on the front page of every paper in the state he would quickly be captured unless he disappeared completely.

To that end he sat down to determine the best way to get away, and he decided that stowing away on a freight train might be his best bet. It would take him miles away without stopping. Knowing generally which direction to go to find the trains, he was on his way when he found himself in a truck yard where three trailers were being loaded.

Seeing the sleepers on the trucks, he determined they were in for a long haul and instead of going on to the trains, he found himself sneaking into the first trailer the minute he had the chance. There was plenty of room to hide even while the men finished loading, and he could only hope that it would be as easy to get away at the other end without being caught.

For hours he stayed hidden away in the stuffy confines of that dark trailer with no food or water, dozing often, yet instantly alert whenever the truck slowed or stopped, questioning often his sanity in getting himself locked inside a trailer from which he couldn't escape until someone opened the door for him. But when the journey was finally over he was again fortunate to make his escape undetected.

As he finally breathed the air of open spaces again it was dusk and he realized he'd spent an entire night and day locked inside the prison of that truck. At first freedom from his confinement was all that had mattered to him, but as he began to relax again and come to his senses he realized he was really starved, and he set out looking for some food.

By then he had two days growth of his beard to disguise him, and apparently that was enough to keep him from being recognized, though the fact that he found himself in Dallas, Texas, twelve hundred miles away may have helped. At any rate, as his hunger seemed to prevent his mind from thinking clearly so that he was no longer so careful about keeping himself hidden, he was surprised to find that no one seemed to give him a second thought.

Like a shameless bum he began scrounging in garbage cans and dumpsters for anything edible, where upon he found an old pair of overalls. Though they had a three-inch rip in the back of the left leg, and were in need of a good washing, they had been a good cover to hide his prison-wear. But they did nothing to fill his stomach, so on he searched.

The smell of food from an open restaurant a few blocks away drew him as his hunger seemed to grow with every passing second, and certain there must be something edible, he was shamelessly digging through the scraps when the back door opened.

Instantly guilt made him jump, then fear of being caught and returned to prison filled him, and finally shame took the place of his fear as he realized the depths to which he had stooped. But the man who had caught him was kind, and again he was fortunate. Realizing that Mike was just hungry, he invited him in, offering him a hot meal in exchange for a couple hours of dish washing.

"If you're interested," said the man who had introduced himself as Terry Mulligan. "I'm in need of a dishwasher on this shift for the rest of the week. The job is yours if you want it."

So he had worked for Terry for the next three nights, receiving one hot meal each night as well as a little money for his services. When the job was over he moved on, not wanting to stay in any place too long in case someone might recognize him. With the beard as a disguise he seemed to blend in, but he was still nervous as he set out looking for a job with which to support himself.

But jobs were scarce, and the ones he could find demanded identification, a social security number, and references he couldn't provide. Even if he had possessed the needed documents he couldn't have produced them without revealing himself and getting sent back to the prison he had worked so hard to avoid.

To make matters worse, everywhere he went it seemed the police were there, watching him, and his own guilty conscience made him certain they were suspicious of his every move. If he wasn't careful it would only be a matter of time before he was caught and returned to California to endure his sentence.

It was then that he left Texas, hitchhiking north for a while. But things didn't change. Still he could get no job without identification and still there appeared to be police everywhere.

Finally, as he could find no other recourse, he had taken to the woods. Spending the very last of his dish washing money on supplies, he set out in search of a secluded spot in the hills where he could build himself some sort of shelter and live off the land and whatever crops he could grow with the seeds he had procured.

For three days he wandered aimlessly through the woods looking for the perfect place until he came across the abandoned cabin. Overgrown with weeds and shrubs, he was certain it had not seen occupants in years, and a careful search of the surrounding area told him it was unlikely anyone would be returning. The road was so overgrown as to be nonexistent in many places. And the nearest hiking trails were miles away. He had made it his home ever since.

"It sounds like you've been pretty fortunate," Penny said when finally his story was finished.

"I guess I have," he agreed. "I may not have a lot here, much of what I do have is borrowed from whoever left it behind. But at least I have shelter, food, water, my freedom–"

"And now you have me," Penny said.

Mike was silent.

"You do have me, Mike," she repeated. "I'm here as your friend for as long as you need me."

"You can't stay, Penny, you know that," he said quietly. "Your family is out there wondering what has happened to you. They need you. They need to know you're okay. You've got to go home."

"I know," she admitted. "As soon as my leg is healed enough to make the trip I'll have to go let them know I'm still alive. But I hate to leave you out here all alone. I… There must be something I can do."

"You've done it, Penny," he said. "You've given me what I haven't had in two years, maybe my entire life. You've given me a reason to go on. You've believed in me without reservation. No one has ever done that before. It's given me a reason to believe in myself. I think the Good Lord sent you to me to remind me of all I do have, and to be grateful for it. I thank you for that, Penny, and I am grateful."

Tears stung Penny's eyes. "I've been fortunate, too," she whispered. "Fortunate to meet a man who is so kind and caring, yet strong enough to deal with all you've been through. And I'm fortunate that you were there to rescue me. I'll never forget you, Mike, not as long as I live."

Chapter Seven

Over the next few days Penny and Mike spent their time preparing her to leave. Neither of them spoke much, knowing that her leaving was inevitable, yet neither wanting to see her leave. Penny worked on her animal-skin garment so as to have something to wear upon her return other than Mike's shirt, not wanting to connect him with her in any way.

She also had to get herself accustomed to walking on her bad leg. Until now the only walking she'd done every day was around the cabin, out to the spring or the outhouse. But to get home she was going to have to walk for hours, maybe even days.

To aid her in her walking Mike found her a good walking stick and she practiced by walking his trap line with him twice every day. As she was unused to walking so much she took her sewing project with her. When she was too tired and sore to go on, usually because she favored her bad leg so much that her good leg felt the strain, she would sit and sew while Mike finished the line. When he returned to her side they would return to the cabin together. Each day she was able to walk a little further, though she still knew walking out of here was going to be a long, difficult journey.

Mike prepared food for their journey, mostly dried meat of one kind or another to give them energy for the trip. Drying the meat took time, though not as long as it took for Penny's leg to grow strong enough to make the trip. But Penny was not in any hurry to go. Despite knowing her family would be terribly worried about her, she hated to leave Mike all alone when he so clearly needed a friend.

Every day Penny practiced walking as far as she could and by the fourth day – a Friday, though they weren't counting – she managed to walk almost half a mile before her good leg got so tired of supporting her as she catered to her bad leg that she felt she had to stop and rest. As usual Mike went on to finish his trap line while she sat to work on her garment.

It was slow work. The skins were small, so it took quite a number of them to make a garment of any size. Having no proper tools for the job made it take that much longer, but with determination and a little creativity she now had a garment that was long enough to cover her most private parts, though it was going to take another day or two to get enough length that she could move with any modesty. Bending over was out completely.

As she sewed she contemplated the fact that the time she and Mike had together was quickly growing more and more limited as her garment neared completion. When it was finished she had to return to her family, at least for a while, to let them know she was alive and well. But leaving him concerned her. After his confiding in her so completely the other night he seemed to relax more, as if he was resigned to the fact that she was going to be his friend whether he wanted her to or not. And yet there was still a reserve in him that made her certain he feared getting too close when he knew she would be going away very soon.

She wanted to stay with him, leaving him all alone out here worried her. Regardless of how well he might have done out here alone for a year before she arrived on the scene, she was certain it wasn't good for him, and she knew it mattered dearly to her what happened to him. It was more than the fact he had saved her life. He was just too good of a person to have to suffer alone like this.

Even so, a part of her continued to hold to the hope that she might be able to find a way to free him of the conviction that held him captive out here. She had to go home eventually, so maybe she could work on finding a way to get him a new trial, find some new evidence to prove his innocence. And yet she knew that was asking a lot. She knew nothing about the law, she knew nothing about his case except what he had told her, and if he and his attorney had found nothing to help him she was unlikely to do so either.

So she wavered between a desire stay with him forever, and a desire to hurry home to find the answers she needed to free him – knowing she really had little hope of achieving success, especially without revealing herself and her relationship to Mike in the process and possibly getting them both into worse trouble than he was in now.

Could she ever forgive herself if she caused him to be sent…?

Her thoughts were interrupted as Mike returned unexpectedly. Immediately his haste and the look on his face told her something was wrong.

"Mike, what is it?" she asked, rising to her feet before he'd even reached her.

"Police."

That one word, spoken in a hoarse whisper, explained clearly his fear. If the authorities found him now there was nothing they could do to keep him out of prison.

"There's several people with them," he said. "One of them is the woman who left you here for dead."

"Caroline?" she said, speaking in the same hoarse whisper that he was using, as if both feared their voices might carry to the enemy beyond. "Then they're looking for me. Turn your back."

"What?"

"Turn your back," she repeated. "They can't find me in your shirt."

He gave her unfinished garment a hurried glance, then obediently turned away while she changed as quickly as possible. Her agitation was clear and, whether he was actually to blame or not, guilt tore at him for endangering her.

"I'm sorry, Penny," he said. "If they find out you've been with me–"

"They won't find out," she promised as she shrugged herself into the half-finished garment. "I won't let them arrest you."

"And what about you?" he asked. "If they know you've been here with me all this time they're going to accuse you of being an accessory, or abetting a fugitive…unless you turn me in, tell them I held you here against your will–"

Finished dressing, she hobbled over in front of him to look up into his face.

"They're not going to know, Mike," she said again. "Even if they did find out we were together – which they won't because I won't let them – it wouldn't affect me. I could claim I had no idea who you were, that you were just the man who saved my life and took care of me until I was strong enough to go home – which would have been true if I hadn't found those clippings. But I won't let them find out. I won't let them send you back to prison. Now let me get rid of these rags around my splint, then you can show me where they are and you can stay out of sight. Once they find me they'll quit looking."

Wordlessly he helped her sit again while they replaced the rags with more strips of animal skin. Then, after handing her the walking stick he'd provided her with earlier, he helped her back to her feet. The rags he put in his pocket rather than leaving them lying around, the shirt he slipped on over the one he was already wearing. Finally he lifted her in his arms.

"Put me down," she ordered. "I can walk, and you've got to stay out of sight."

"I will," he said as he began carrying her in the direction from which he had just come. "But it is quite a ways down there and we can move faster if I carry you."

He did move fast, even with her in his arms he was hurrying faster than she ever could have walked on her bad leg, but it was still several minutes before he stopped and set her on the ground.

"They're down there," he said in a whisper, pointing over the edge of the bluffs through the trees.

From that point she could see both the spot by the road on the bluff across the river where Caroline had attacked her and the narrow river below. Parked in the place Caroline had parked three weeks earlier there now stood a police car, Robert's Jaguar, and her parent's mini van. Alongside the river bank below were a number of people apparently searching the ground for clues – two police officers, both of her parents, all of her brothers and sisters, Caroline, and Robert.

Had Caroline had an attack of conscience? Had she confessed her crime? Was that why they were here now? Had they come searching for her dead body?

But Penny had no time for speculation. She had to get to them and get them out of here before they had a chance to learn about Mike. And one of those officers was getting far too interested in something he saw there on the ground.

"How do I get down from here?" he asked Mike in a barely audible whisper.

He indicated a spot to her left where the ground sloped down. "Be careful," he whispered back. "It's steep."

"You stay out of sight," she cautioned.

She turned away, but she had only taken one step when an impulse made her turn back. On the tip toe of her good foot she reached up to kiss his mouth.

"I'll never forget you," she whispered. And then she was gone.

In a state of shock Mike stood watching her until she was out of his sight down the slope of the hill. She would never forget him? He wondered just how true that would prove to be. Since he would never see her again he would never know for sure, but once she was back with her family and friends her memory of him would likely fade rapidly. He, however, would never forget her as long as he lived.

The taste of her kiss lingered on his mouth and he savored its glory as he looked down through the trees on the people below, the people who had come to take her away from him. He couldn't hear from this distance what they were saying over the sounds of the forest around him, but they were clearly very concerned for her. Caroline, the woman who had tried to kill her, seemed terribly confused and worried – probably because the body she had expected to find was missing.

Penny was still out of his sight on her decent toward them when a sudden impulse sent him after her. He wouldn't let her or anyone else see him. He would just make sure she made it safely, that she didn't fall on her way down or anything.

He caught sight of her just as she reached the bottom of the hill. The curve of the land there prevented the others from seeing her just yet, and he saw her stop just a foot or so from the water's edge. Balancing on one foot, her walking stick leaning against her leg, she used both hands to muss her hair. She then bent to get a bit of dry dirt from the ground at her feet which she rubbed into her hair, on the fur garment she had made, and on the skin of her face, arms and legs. She didn't over do it. Just enough to erase the evidence that she'd had the use of a comb or a wash cloth out here.

She looked the part she wished to portray perfectly as she started hobbling along again on her walking stick. Mike kept to the trees to avoid being seen as he followed her, getting close enough to see and hear her reunion with the others as she rounded the corner without being spotted.

"Daddy!"

Instantly at the sound of her voice every eye was on her. They seemed all to be in shock for a long second, then many of them were running toward her, throwing their arms around her as they all cried with joy. Those on the other side of the river rushed right through the water without any concern about how soaked they were to their knees or higher.

Only four of the people he saw did not rush to her side. The two officers took their time, waiting for the reunion to relax a bit before joining in. Caroline stood rooted to the spot as if she thought she was seeing a ghost and was too terrified to move.

The other person who didn't rush to Penny's side was a man who seemed filled with deep emotions at the sight of her yet possibly felt his attentions would be unwelcome. It was apparent to Mike from his hiding place among the bushes and trees that this man was in love with Penny, and jealousy stung at his heart.

Was this Robert? If so, how would Penny respond to his being here in this search for her? Would she realize that the man was in love with her after all? Would that be enough for her to give him another chance? Deep inside was the worst pain Mike had ever known as he realized just how easily she would forget him now that she was back in her own world with those who loved her.

But it was only right that she did, he reminded himself. He could offer her nothing. And for her to remember him as he would remember her would only bring her the same heartache he knew would be his for the rest of his life. She deserved better than that. It was only right that she find real love and happiness with someone worthy of her.

Everyone was talking at once at first, and Penny just hugged her family as they all wept tears of surprise and joy together.

"Are you okay!"

"We were so worried!"

"We thought we would never see you again!"

"When we got that anonymous note saying we would find your body here we thought there was no hope."

An anonymous note? Had Caroline sent them a note so they would learn what she had done without incriminating herself? As the sentiments continued flowing Mike felt the urge to go out there and strangle the woman who had hurt his Penny so seriously without any remorse. It was only the knowledge that she was now safe again with her family and that their having any knowledge of his presence with her would cause her more trouble than help that kept him rooted to the spot.

"Honey, we've been so worried," the man who was clearly her father said, finally getting his chance to speak. "What happened?"

This time the others all waited for her answer, as if he bore enough authority to demand an answer that no one else had waited for in their own questioning. Penny didn't answer immediately, but looked to the one woman who was still rooted to the spot some fifty feet from them.

"Maybe you should ask Caroline that," she suggested in a quiet tone that Mike could barely hear.

"Caroline?"

Clearly they were all confused by that, but one look at Caroline's face told them just how involved she had been and panic seemed to overtake her as they all stared at her.

"It wasn't my fault!" she said, suddenly wild with desperation. "I didn't want to hurt you! They made me! If I didn't keep you from marrying Robert they were going to send me to prison for stealing that one stupid ring! I couldn't go to prison! I couldn't! I just couldn't! I had to keep you from marrying Robert!"

"My parents put you up to this?" asked the man Mike had already determined was Robert.

"I only wanted to borrow the ring!" Caroline said, frantic now. "But they caught me! But they said they wouldn't prosecute me if I kept you from marrying Robert! I couldn't go to prison! I couldn't! If you married Robert I would go to prison!"

"Caroline, Robert and I had already broken up," Penny said, looking at the man in question, though her back was to Mike so he could not see her expression. "Why would you think…?"

"He changed his mind!" Caroline ranted like a crazy person. "He changed his mind, and they were going to send me to prison just because I took one ring. I only wanted to borrow it and they said I stole it. And they were going to have me arrested if I didn't help them. I didn't want to do it. I didn't want to hurt you. I'm so sorry, Penny. I'm so sorry."

Her hysterical ranting turned to hysterical crying and as she sank to the ground one of the officers went to her side. The woman was obviously deranged to have decided killing her friend was the only way to keep her from marrying someone, that killing her friend was better than going to prison. For a moment her hysterical confession stunned everyone else into silence.

"I take it you're Penny Loftin?" the other officer asked Penny as Caroline continued sobbing apologies in his partner's arms.

"I am," Penny agreed.

Loftin. Penny Loftin. It was the first time Mike had heard her surname. Not knowing it hadn't seemed to matter before, but now he realized how good it felt to know that added little detail about her – though a pain shot through his breast at the thought that if Robert wanted to marry her after all it wasn't likely to stay Loftin for long.

"Can you tell us exactly what happened and how Miss Bower is involved?" the officer asked Penny.

Mike held his breath as he waited for her explanation. He was certain she would never purposely hurt him, but would she be able to convince them of her story without involving him?

Penny stood leaning against her father, his arm around her on one side while her mother's arms both held her on the other side as if she feared she might disappear again any second. Everyone gave her their full attention as they awaited her story, everyone but Caroline and the officer to whom she continued to sob.

"Caroline asked me to go for a drive with her," she explained. "She said she wanted to talk, and since it was a Sunday afternoon I had the time so I agreed. We did that kind of thing fairly often. Anyway, we drove for two or three hours just talking. Then, just as the sun was going down, she stopped the car up there where your cars are parked. She said she wanted to look at the view, but as we stood looking out over the river and the valley beyond she suddenly struck me from behind, saying she was sorry as she did so, and the next thing I knew I was waking up in those bushes there – stark naked."

As Penny told her story her mother gasped in shock and the others all looked just as astonished as they measured the distance of her fall with their eyes, knowing it was a miracle she hadn't been killed on impact.

"Penny, why didn't you get in touch with us?" her father asked.

Her mother added, "That was three weeks ago. We've been worried to death not hearing from you, not knowing what had happened to you. And this morning we got this note…"

"Three weeks?" Penny asked, as if the elapsed time was a surprise to her. "I had no idea it was so long. I guess because at first I didn't remember what had happened. I didn't even remember who I was. I seemed to come in and out of consciousness for a long time, and even after that I was just functioning on pure instinct. My leg hurt, so I splinted it, I was hungry, so I trapped a rabbit or a squirrel like Dad taught us up at the cabin…"

"You ate it raw?" That question came from one of the teenage girls Mike knew to be her sister, though he wasn't quite sure which one she would be.

"Of course not, silly," Penny said with an affectionate hug to her younger sister. "Daddy taught us to make fire with sticks. I couldn't seem to remember who I was or where I was, but an instinct for survival seemed to make me remember all of your training."

She said that last as she turned to her father, giving him a hug, and Mike was aware she was telling the truth about that. She had acted on instinct in the beginning. Even without knowing her he had been aware that it was the instinct of forgotten experiences that had motivated her every action from the start.

"So I guess I have you to thank for my still being here, don't I?" she said, smiling at her father. But he did not return her smile.

"You do remember now?" he asked.

"I remember," she assured him. "Little things kept coming back to me one at a time – mostly memories of our vacations in the woods. But a couple nights ago I had a nightmare that seemed to bring everything back with a crash. Then my only problems were a way to cover my birthday suit and finding my way out of here. I was working on this–"

With a laugh she indicated the fur garment she was wearing.

"…when I saw you all down here. It's not much, I feel pretty certain bending over would be a bad idea–"

At that point Robert removed his long-sleeved dress shirt and handed it to her. "Maybe this will help," he said, and Mike felt the pangs of jealousy rip through him again as Penny gave the man a smile of gratitude.

"Thank you, Robert," she said as she tied it by the sleeves around her waist to add length to her present garment. "And if nobody minds, I'd really like to go home to a nice hot shower, some real food, and my own bed."

At her words they all began moving off, talking animatedly about Penny's adventure and their own fears as they went. One of the officers suggested she should get a thorough exam at the hospital and maybe a good night's sleep, but then they would like her to make a full statement at the police station.

As the two officers escorted Caroline between them up across the river toward the hill Penny hobbled along with her family. She had only taken half a dozen steps, though, before Robert said, "Maybe it would be easier if I carried you."

Again the green-eyed monster bit at Mike's heart, but to his delight Penny turned him down.

"Thanks, Robert," she said. "But I can make it."

"No, he's right," the older of her brothers said. "You should stay off that leg as much as possible until you've had it x-rayed."

With that he lifted her in his arms despite her protests, adding as he did so, "Humor your big brother, would you?"

So Penny did just that, wrapping her arms around her brother's neck as she said, "Thanks, David. I'd forgotten how nice it is to have a big brother to look out for me."

As they moved away from him it grew harder and harder for Mike to hear what they were saying. But he stayed where he was. To follow them across the river would be to reveal himself to them and get, not just himself, but Penny in trouble. It was several minutes before they reached the road, and then he watched them drive away – Penny in the van with her sisters and her parents, Robert and her brothers in the Jaguar, and Caroline with the officers in the State Trooper's car.

It was over. Penny was safe again with her family. There was no longer any reason for Mike to stay where he was. Slowly he turned to retrace his steps to his lonely cabin, to curse the powers that had brought a pretty Penny into his life only to take her away again forever.

For Penny the next few days were filled with attention and activity from all sides. The hospital gave her a thorough examination, put her leg in a proper plaster cast – which Penny found more annoying then helpful as her foot kept swelling with no place to go, and any itch was impossible to reach – but otherwise they declared her fit and sent her home.

The morning after her return she made a complete police report on what had happened to her, a story that was nearly the truth, leaving out only the fact that Mike had been with her, taking such good care of her in his cabin rather than her being out in the woods all alone without proper shelter. No one questioned the validity of her story, they were only too happy to have her back safe and sound to even notice if there were any flaws to the story she took such care in telling them.

The attorney Caroline's parents hired for her arranged for her to receive psychiatric help rather than prosecution, at least for the present. And Penny took an afternoon to visit her for the purpose of telling her she was forgiven, though she knew she could never see Caroline as a friend again even if she was mentally ill.

The attentions of her family and friends were non-stop. For the first few days she stayed with her parents, at her mother's insistence, and their phone rang continually with concerned friends wanting confirmation that she was really okay. Many of them also stopped by with gifts and cards and flowers as if she was an invalid – all wanting to hear the story of all that she had been through. The telling of the story got to be so routine she could repeat it over and over again like a tape machine, but she was always careful to concentrate as she spoke so she never let anything slip that might give Mike away.

Roy Loftin was due to make a business trip to Los Angeles the next week, a trip that he had actually canceled when his daughter disappeared. But on her safe return he rescheduled it and, as the attention on Penny seemed to increase with time rather than decreasing, she talked him into taking her with him, something he was perfectly pleased to do.

For Penny, though, there was more than one reason for going to California with her father. From the moment she'd left Mike he had remained on her mind. That kiss she'd given him on departing had been a crazy impulse, but it also served to make her instantly aware of feelings she had not until then put into words.

In the beginning she had not thought about him much at all. She had only known she felt comfortable and safe with him in a way that had been so very important as she survived on only her instincts. Later she had felt gratitude toward him for saving her life, and for all the things he'd done to protect and care for her. Finally, upon learning his secret she had felt sorry for him for all the pain and suffering he'd had to endure all alone for so long.

But that kiss had awakened in her new feelings as well, feelings that had been growing inside her from the beginning but which she hadn't recognized until that moment. Suddenly, with all her heart, she realized she was in love with Mike as she had never been with anyone else. Suddenly she knew it was not just worry about Mike that made her reluctant to leave him. The emptiness inside her was due to a part of her heart being torn from her chest to stay with him forever.

Being so completely in love had taken her by surprise, and it was hard to endure all the compassion and concern of her friends and family when the man she loved was so alone. Until she cleared his name she would never be able to settle to anything else. Whatever happened to her, however long it took, she had to do all she could to give him back his life.

It was because of her new found love more than anything else that she refused Robert when he proposed to her again shortly after her return. Despite the fact that he declared he would never love anyone else and that he no longer cared whether his parents disinherited him or not, she knew she could never care for him the way she did for Mike, and never would she settle for second best now that she knew the deep feelings of really loving someone.

It was for all those reasons she was glad to leave home for a while. And Riverside, Mike's home, was within taxi distance of Los Angeles. She was determined to learn all she could about his case so that she could find a way to prove his innocence. He deserved that, not only because he was innocent of the crime of which they had convicted him, but also because he was a good, kind, wonderful man, the man she would love for the rest of her life. Even if he should never return her feelings she owed him every effort she had to give.

Caution was a must, though. No one must know of her interest in Mike and his case. Any awareness of a connection between them would lead anyone to the conclusion that she must know him, and it wouldn't take much of a guess to learn where they had met. It made no difference to herself if anyone should figure that out, whatever happened to her was of no consequence, but she could never do anything to hurt Mike. To risk sending him back to prison was a gamble she could not take.

While her father attended to business on that Monday morning, just over a week after her return to her family, Penny's first task was to visit the public library in search of the microfilm copies of all newspapers in the area for the past two years. Surely there were other clippings besides those Mike had that would shed some light on the case against him, on the trial and the witnesses and anything else that might help her get a clearer picture of where to go from there.

For hours she sat studying every word in dozens of articles, but not one helpful clue presented itself to bring her nearer to the truth. Besides the two articles of which she'd found copies in the cabin, she also found a number of articles about his arrest, about the trial and the conviction. She saw the depth of betrayal Mike must have felt as everyone doubted his innocence, the comments of those calling themselves his friends clearly showing that even they had believed him guilty in the face of the evidence against him.

Despite the hopelessness of her task she poured through every article of every paper from the first mention of his arrest until the reports of his escape – including hints that his brother, Joe was being watched in case Mike should get in touch with him. But finally she could find nothing more, though she continued looking for a couple months after the last mention just in case something new had turned up.

"Find what you're looking for?"

The masculine voice behind her was just a whisper as fitting for use in a library, but it startled her so intensely that she jumped in her chair while turning immediately to face a short, stocky man in his mid- to late-forties.

"Did you want to use the machine?" she asked as she switched off the light and removed the sheet of microfilm with as much calm as she could maintain so as not to appear suspicious.

"No, you go ahead, Miss…" the man said.

Clearly he was expecting her to supply her name, but she had no intention of doing so. Without knowing who the man was or why he cared if she had found what she was looking for she could take no chances in his learning who she was, especially as he seemed to be showing her more than a casual interest.

"Dick Rabin," he said, holding out his hand which she did not take. "Reporter for the L.A. News Flash. Do you happen to know Michael Klotski?"

"Michael who?" Penny asked as innocently as possible. The last thing she needed was a reporter linking her with Mike, regardless of the depth of the man's curiosity.

The reporter gave a scoffing laugh. "Michael Klotski," he said. "The man whose story you've been researching here for the last four hours. I take it you know where he is."

It was not a question, though doubtlessly it was a shot in the dark, hoping for confirmation from her that she was determined not to give.

"I have no idea what you're talking about," she said as she gathered the microfilms back into their box and got to her feet. "And I must go. If you will excuse me–"

"And just where has he been hiding all this time?" the man insisted, clearly not believing her innocence for a second. It took all her effort not to let the panic she felt sweeping through her to take her over.

"I have no idea what you're talking about," she repeated. "Excuse me."

But he didn't give up. "You do know what I'm talking about," he insisted as he followed her to return the microfilms. "If you'll get me an interview with him I will make it worth your while."

"Just exactly what is a reporter doing spying on people in the library?" Penny asked, hoping to put him on the defensive.

But it did no good. With a grin he said, "I come to do some research and I find a very pretty girl doing the most intense research. Naturally my curiosity is peaked. So tell me about Klotski."

With a frown Penny ignored him. Denying the truth was not convincing the man of anything, but neither could she admit knowing Mike without bringing him harm. If only she had left things alone. Mike may be all alone out there in the forest cabin, but at least he was free. If this reporter learned who she was he would keep looking until he found Mike, and she would rather die than let that happen.

"So, what is your interest in the story?" the man asked as he followed her toward the door.

"My interest is my business," Penny said, walking out of the building, closing the door between them.

But the man did not give up. As it was now after two o'clock and Penny had neglected to take a break for lunch or to put her foot up, she was both starved and uncomfortable with her leg swollen inside the cast. But with the reporter following her she didn't dare return to the hotel until she lost him. Instead she hailed a cab, without any difficulty, and sat back to decide what she could do now.

"Where to, Lady?" the driver asked.

"Somewhere that serves a great lunch at two in the afternoon, and where a girl in a cast can put her foot up," she said with a smile she hoped was calm and friendly without reflecting her worries.

He named a couple places without any enthusiasm and she said, "Whichever is closest. I'm starved."

She then sat back in the seat where she could see a reflection in the rear view mirror of the reporter following in a nondescript gray sedan. Mike was right, she thought with a deep sense of guilt. Just her simple act of reading the old newspapers in the library had the press anxious to pursue her. Just that simple act had increased Mike's danger of re-arrest one hundred percent, and she had no idea how to prevent it from happening.

Chapter Eight

Desperately concerned that her attempt to help Mike had put him in further jeopardy, Penny sat in the homey little café where the cab had dropped her trying to come up with a solution to keep it from getting any worse. The reporter did not enter the café when she did, probably because he was convinced that she would tell him nothing anyway. But he had not given up. He was parked right outside where he could watch her when she left.

In an attempt to avoid having him watch her eat she took a table as far back from the window as possible and took her time over her sandwich and salad while she tried to come up with an effective method of losing her shadow before he managed to discover who she really was. As much as she wanted to help Mike gain his freedom, she knew she had made a terrible mistake in showing any interest in him at all and now she had to lose the reporter before she made things any worse.

So how did they lose shadows in the movies? Find a back door near the rest rooms maybe. She could sneak out the back door, find another cab, and disappear before the reporter knew she was gone. After catching the attention of the waitress she paid the bill and the tip with cash without leaving her table. If the reporter saw her near the windows paying her bill he would know she was leaving and wonder why she didn't come out.

Having done that she asked the woman where the rest rooms were and hobbled back there in her casted foot to make her escape unobserved. But to her disappointment there was no back door in sight, not even a door to the kitchen, just a tiny little alcove with two rest rooms leading off of it.

Disappointed she tried to come up with another solution. Maybe if she caught another cab to the bus station or the airport. Maybe she could convince the man she was leaving town for some completely irrelevant destination and lose him there.

As she caught another cab she tried to work out just how to go about that deception without making her tail suspicious. The bus station seemed the best bet. It wouldn't involve as much walking on her bad leg as the airport would. Besides, she really would be taking a plane home when she and her father left in a couple days. Maybe this would keep him from discovering that fact as well.

The driver of that cab was a heavyset woman, probably nearing sixty, with a pleasant smile who cheerfully drove her in the direction of the Greyhound Station while making small talk about the weather and her fare's cast. Only a few minutes later, though, she interrupted herself in mid-sentence to comment, "I think there's someone following you."

Penny sighed. "I know," she admitted without turning around to look.

The woman glanced at her in the mirror. "Who is he?"

"A reporter," Penny confessed. She didn't really want to tell this woman anything, but in the light of her obvious concern she felt it would be unkind not to say something.

"You someone famous?" the woman asked, glancing again at her as if to try and decide whether she'd ever seen her before or not.

"No," Penny said.

But feeling certain the woman didn't believe her, and fearing the reporter might catch up with this woman later with his questions, she decided what she needed was a good story, one that would satisfy this woman and the reporter both.

"I just happen to know someone famous," she said. "And the reporter insists on bothering me about him."

The woman moved her eyes from the road to her fare a couple of times while Penny tried to think of a good story. Suddenly a smile filled the driver's face.

"Someone you're in love with," she said. "So are you going to marry the guy?"

Startled by the woman's perception, Penny stared at her. She was in love with Mike, but she had not been aware that it showed so clearly to total strangers. Was that what the reporter had seen as well? Was that why he was so determined to follow her?

"So you want to lose this guy?" the woman asked. She clearly saw the romance of the situation and was ready to give the story a happy ending if at all possible.

"Can you do that?" Penny asked. It was more like a movie than any experience Penny had ever expected to undergo.

"Watch me," the woman said with a sense of excitement in her voice.

For several blocks she continued on as usual, nonchalant, just casually driving a fare to a regular stop. But suddenly, just in front of a string of five or six cars, she whipped the car across two lanes to make a left hand turn into a side street. In surprise Penny turned to watch the reporter. But he had to wait for the string of cars before following. By then the cab had turned left again, then right, then another left, and was driving in a completely different direction from before. For several blocks Penny watched the street behind, but the reporter's car never reappeared.

"Amateurs," the woman said with satisfaction.

Penny thanked her whole-heartedly. "I've been trying for an hour to figure out how to lose that man," she added. "But wearing a cast kind of slows a person down."

"Well, you've lost him now," the woman said with pride at her achievement. "But don't count on him staying lost if he knows who you are."

"He doesn't know," Penny said. "That's part of his reason for following me. He knows I'm the woman in Mike's life, but that's all he knows and he wants to know more. He wants to play up the sentimental angle that Mike's found love after all he's been through."

"He's been through a lot, has he?" the woman asked with all the curiosity Penny would have shown in her place.

Knowing that it was likely the reporter would later come looking for this woman for information, Penny decided sticking partly to the truth would be more confusing and convincing than a complete lie, though without the time to think it all through carefully she feared saying all the wrong things. Still, she had to say something.

"It's a long story," Penny said, calming some as her mind began racing with ideas to spice it up. "And it was in the past. I just wish they would leave it alone now – at least until after the wedding."

Okay, so there wasn't really going to be a wedding. At least not as things stood for Mike right now. Even if he should feel as she did, he would never ask her to marry him while he was a fugitive. But it was clearly a good story with which to interest her cab driver, and even if the reporter should learn of it, there would be no record of Mike marrying anyone that he could exploit for his story. Nor would it hurt Mike if he never learned of it in his far away hideout.

"After the wedding they can do as they please," she continued. "I just want a quiet little wedding, not a media circus."

"Understandable," the woman said with sympathy, though clearly still curious. "So, do you still want to go to the Greyhound station?"

Penny thought about it and changed her mind. For effect she gave a careful look at the new wristwatch her father had given her to replace the one Caroline had removed from her wrist before pushing her over the bluff.

"Now that I've lost my shadow it doesn't much matter," she said. "I was only going to go there to try and confuse him, make him think I was leaving town. Now I guess I could go ahead and finish what I started to do. Maybe you could take me to the Sweet Eternity Wedding Chapel."

The Sweet Eternity was a quaint little chapel behind the hotel where she and her father were staying. Penny had noticed it particularly because she could see it from her room and she had thought it looked sweetly romantic. It seemed the perfect place to go now. It was close enough to the hotel she could sneak back there after the cab dropped her off, and it fit in perfectly with her story. The driver's knowing smile confirmed it. The thought that her pretty, young fare and her fiancé were to be married there was just the right romantic touch Penny's story needed.

"Would you like me to wait?" the driver asked as she pulled up in front of the chapel a few minutes later.

Penny gave her a smile and a big tip. "Thank you," she said. "But I'll be a while. There are so many arrangements to make—"

The woman wished her luck, but as Penny started up the beautiful flower-lined path to the front door she realized there was a string of traffic preventing the cab from leaving and to avoid looking suspicious she had to enter the building even though she had not actually planned to do so.

"May I help you?" a cheerful, friendly young woman asked before she had even closed the door behind her.

"Uh, no…well…"

A quick glance through the window showed the cab to still be there. She was trapped.

"Well, yes, maybe, I hope so," she said to stall for time. "I would like to schedule a wedding."

The cab finally pulled out into the street to drive away.

"Certainly," the woman said as she pulled an open date book close in front of her. "Would you and your fiancé prefer an altar ceremony or a garden ceremony?"

"A garden ceremony," Penny said, not that it mattered since she wasn't really getting married, but the idea of a garden ceremony did have a certain appeal.

"Wonderful," the woman said cheerfully. "And what date did you have in mind?"

Penny thought quickly. "Saturday?"

"Oh dear, I'm sorry," the woman said. "We are really booked this Saturday. We do have one opening on Friday at two o'clock. Or, let's see…Sunday…no, we're booked solid all weekend."

"What about for an altar ceremony?" Penny asked in keeping with the story she had been living all afternoon, as if she really was a bride-to-be making wedding plans.

"I'm sorry," the woman said. "We have only one minister available at any one time. He can perform an altar ceremony or a garden ceremony, but not both at the same time, of course."

She turned a page in her book, then another.

"We do have several openings during the week," she continued. "But on the weekends…nothing for two weeks. I'm sorry. Would another day be okay?"

"I would have to discuss that with my fiancé," Penny said, grateful for the excuse not to make an appointment after all, even if it would be one that was never kept.

"Certainly," the woman said with apology in her eyes. "We also do evening services. We don't have an opening there until eight o'clock next Monday, but we would be glad to fit you and your fiancé in then if you would like."

"Thank you," Penny said. "But I really should speak to him before deciding. He may prefer the Friday at two slot."

"Certainly," the woman said again. "Why don't you leave your name…"

She reached for a business card from the dispenser on her desk as she spoke.

"…and when you've spoken to your fiancé just give me a call. My name is Cindy."

"Thank you," Penny said, accepting the card without giving her name.

"And your name is…?" Cindy urged gently.

Having no wish to leave her real name just in case the cab driver or the reporter should follow her trail to this place, she made one up off the top of her head.

"Denise," she said, citing the name of her cousin's wife. "Spears," the name of her favorite professor in college.

"Denise Spears," the woman repeated as she made a note of it. "Very well, I shall be looking forward to your call."

Penny thanked her, but as she prepared to leave she noticed a taxi parked across the street. She wasn't sure if it was the same one in which she had arrived or not – she couldn't see the driver and she had paid no attention to the number – but just in case she decided it would be best not to leave just yet. She wasn't about to let anyone follow her to the hotel, and she was tired of the chase game she'd been playing all this time. She turned back to Cindy.

"I don't suppose it would be possible for me to see the garden where the ceremony would take place?"

"Of course," Cindy agreed, getting to her feet. "Mr. Stevens is in the middle of an altar ceremony at the moment, but the garden is free. And if you would like to wait you could meet him and our organist. We also have a very good photographer…"

"Thank you," Penny said. "But I do need to meet my fiance in a few minutes. If I could just see the garden for a moment, maybe we could meet everybody in another day or so."

"Of course," Cindy said again as she led the way through the front office, down a wide hall past a room on the left where the faint hum of voices could be heard and three doors on the right marked 'His', 'Hers', and 'Private.'

Finally they stepped out through a door at the end into a beautiful garden. At one end of a perfectly manicured lawn stood a heart-shaped, white trellis on a white platform standing six inches off the ground. Otherwise there was nothing there to suggest that it was anything but an ordinary garden to some expensive mansion somewhere.

"We can decorate the front there in any colors you choose," Cindy said as they walked in that direction. "We usually line up the chairs for the guests along here so you're able to make a grand and traditional entrance."

She smiled and Penny returned her smile. The place was beautiful – perfect for a wedding, but she was beginning to feel a bit uncomfortable with all the deception. Talking of weddings made her wish all the more that she and Mike were really getting married, but that was only a dream, at least at this point, and the sooner she got her head out of the clouds the better.

If she was ever to have even a chance of a relationship with Mike she had to first find a way to free him from the conviction so wrongly imposed on him. Even if he should feel anything for her he would never jeopardize her in any way by even suggesting such a thing until then. Even then she would have to convince him that taking such a chance was worth the effort. After the way his wife had mistreated him he may not be so willing to take a chance on being hurt again – even if he did feel anything.

"I'm sorry," Penny said, suddenly coming out of her thoughts as she realized Cindy had been talking to her while her own thoughts wandered. "What were you saying?"

Cindy smiled, a knowing smile, as if she was used to brides-to-be daydreaming as they looked over the grounds. "I hope our garden is satisfactory."

"Oh, it is," Penny assured her while pushing away the feelings of guilt for wasting the poor woman's time. "I was just thinking how perfect it is – so beautiful and...romantic."

"We think so," Cindy said, not without pride. "Of course you will want to make certain arrangements of your own – your choice of flowers, music, possibly many things. But we can easily help you arrange all that if you desire. And if you will let us know how many guests there will be we will set up the chairs for you."

Reluctantly Penny came back to reality, out of the fantasy of her own making. She was not really getting married. Out of a desire to protect Mike's interests she was wasting Cindy's time, and getting carried away with herself in the process. What she should really be doing was getting out of here, back to the hotel before she made things worse than they already were.

"Thank you, Cindy," she said. "I will have to let you know all the details later. But right now I really should be going."

"Certainly," Cindy said. "Just give us a call. If you call after four I won't be here, but I'll leave word with Tanya and she'll help you."

Penny thanked her again. Then, indicating a gate between the shrubs at the side of the garden – her perfect back-door escape – asked, "Is it possible to go out that way? My car is parked on that side of the block, and with this cast the less walking I have to do the better."

Cindy smiled. "Sure," she said as she pulled a ring of keys from a pocket and led the way to the gate in question. "How much longer will you be in the cast?"

Clearly she was thinking in terms of the wedding she believed Penny to be planning and Penny smiled. "Too long. But I'll find a way to get down that aisle if it kills me."

With a laugh Cindy unlocked and opened the gate, stepping aside to let Penny pass. "Well, good luck," she said. "And let us know if there is anything we can do to make it easier for you. We're here to help."

Penny thanked her again, then bid her goodbye and slowly started walking toward a little red sedan parked at the curb. As soon as the gate closed behind her, however, she turned, double checked to see that no one was watching her, and finally was able to return to the hotel to wait for her father, fretting and worrying about all that she had done and miserable to think she may have caused Mike more harm than good.

It was six o'clock when Roy Loftin returned to the hotel. His business had gone well, but his mind was not on his success. Rather, it was on his daughter as he opened the door to their suite. From the moment they had found her out there in the woods and brought her home there had been something unquestionably different about her. In many ways she seemed sad and lost, as if something important was missing from her life now. At others he felt she was worried, even a little frightened about something.

Undoubtedly all that she had been through – both the shock of Caroline attacking her and the hardships she must have endured for three weeks all alone out there with only her wits to save her – would have lasting consequences, and maybe it was more the regrets and the fears she felt at being treated so cruelly by a trusted friend than anything else which left her feeling so uncertain and unhappy. But something inside him, a fatherly instinct he had developed so strongly over the years, made him fear that it was something more, something she had not yet confided in him, possibly something more than she even remembered, that controlled her now.

With those thoughts on his mind he was not surprised as he entered the suite to find her sitting by the window in the main room, staring moodily down at the chapel gardens below, her casted foot resting on a pillow on a chair in front of her while deep in the thoughts that troubled her.

"Penny?" he spoke as she turned her face to give him a smile of greeting. "How was your day?"

"It was okay," she said with more promise in her tone than in her eyes. "How was yours? Did you get the contract?"

"We got it," he said with a frown.

Again she was changing the subject. Ever since her return from that place in the woods she had done her best to avoid talking about her feelings or her experience. It was that avoidance that concerned him most. Whether it was deliberate or unconscious he hadn't decided, but it wasn't good. And now that they were alone he intended to get to the bottom of it, one way or another.

"Mr. Braynard liked your proposal, then," she said.

"He liked it," Roy said. "But I don't want to talk about business just now, Penny. I want to talk about you."

"Me?" she asked, as if surprised at the request, though he did not miss the guarded look that filled her eyes. He was going to have to proceed carefully but firmly.

"You," he said. "I want to know what you did today. You didn't just sit here staring out the window all day, I hope."

She gave him a smile, a smile he recognized. It said that, yes, she had gone out, but either he was not going to like what she had done, or his knowing what she had done was going to embarrass her. In an attempt to get her to relax he lifted her leg and the pillow so that he could sit on the chair they were occupying rather than towering over her.

"Just what did you do today?" he asked as he placed the pillow and her leg down on his lap.

Her smile was one of obvious embarrassment now. "Mostly I made a fool of myself."

Keeping his voice light and yet fatherly he asked, "And just how did you manage to do that?"

For a moment he thought she was not going to give him an answer as she sat staring out through the window. It seemed she was struggling with her thoughts, debating whether or not to tell him what was on her mind and he debated just how far to press her. He wanted desperately to know everything that bothered her, but he knew from experience pushing would most likely have the opposite effect.

For a long moment she was silent and he contented himself with massaging the toes at the end of her cast as he waited. But when she did speak he was still not certain it was much of an answer.

"You see that little chapel down there?" she asked.

He saw it. He nodded.

"The garden there would be a perfect place for a wedding, don't you think?"

The wistful look in her eyes as she stared down at that garden made him suddenly aware that whatever was on her mind involved the deepest feelings of her heart – love as he had not seen in her before.

"Have you and Robert changed your minds again?" he asked, trying to decipher her thoughts. "Are you getting married after all?"

Again she turned her smile on him as she reached over to place her hand over his that now rested on her cast.

"No, Daddy," she said. "It's over for good between me and Robert. Robert suggested we give it another try, and I think he would genuinely try to make it work this time, but I just…it just wouldn't work. I realize that now."

"Then there is someone else."

That had to be it. He knew her too well to believe otherwise.

"Come on, Honey," he said when she turned back to the window rather than answering him. "I know something has been bothering you ever since we found you out there in the woods. Whatever it is, you know you can talk to me about it."

She continued to stare out through the window, but he could see she was wanting to confide in him. Gently he placed his other hand over hers, which still covered his, and she turned her eyes to his.

"Daddy, if I tell you something, will you promise never to breath a word of it to a living soul? Not even to Mama?"

He didn't like the sound of that, the seriousness of a request like she had never made before.

"Penny, you know your mother would never break your confidence any more than I would."

"I know," she said. "But she would worry. And she can't hide her worries."

Roy stared at his daughter. She was serious. A sense of pride filled him to think she should feel such confidence in him as to reveal something so terribly important that she couldn't share it with another person. Yet such a request also filled him with concern. Whatever was bothering her must be affecting her deeply to make such a request and he worried what could be so momentous to the daughter he loved so dearly.

"Alright, Honey," he promised. "If that's the way you want it, I won't say anything to anyone, not even your mother. But you must let me help you in any way I can."

"Thank you, Daddy," she said, squeezing his hand. But she stared out through the window again before going on. "Daddy–"

Her pause was far too long, but he resisted the urge to rush her, just caressed her hand and waited while she stared blindly through the window.

"I wasn't…completely honest with you about what happened after Caroline…tried to kill me."

At last. He'd known something of serious importance was missing from her story, but he had been unsure how to approach her about it. Now at last she was revealing it to him. He must be sure to respond to all she told him the way she needed him to respond in order help her through whatever difficulties she was struggling with.

"Mostly I told you the truth," she said after what seemed an endless pause in which he held her hand and tried to be patient, to let her reveal her story in her own way. "I just…I left out one detail."

She stopped and looked at him, begging him with her eyes. "You promise you won't say anything…?"

He squeezed her hand again, his heart heavy and anxious over the fact that whatever was bothering her should make her need his promise again.

"Honey, you know I would never repeat anything you told me

without your permission," he promised again. "I give you my word that I won't say anything to anyone, not even your mother if that is how you want it. You have my promise."

"I'm sorry, Daddy," she said, sensing that his pride was feeling a bit wounded. "It's just that it's not my secret. It's…I wasn't alone out there. I came to, just like I told you, without knowing who I was or where I was. But I wasn't in the bushes. I was in a cabin. The man who lived there had found me. He saved my life. He saved my life, Daddy. And he did so at the risk of his own."

So this was the man who had put the worry into her eyes, Roy thought. His daughter had been alone with some strange man for three weeks. What had he done to her? What awful things had he done to her to make her afraid even to admit knowing him?

But it was imperative that he keep his voice calm. That was what she needed from him now – calm, patient understanding. "Who was this man?" he asked. "Did he…hurt you?"

"No, Daddy," she assured him, her eyes pleading with him to believe her. "He didn't hurt me in any way. He saved my life. I was unconscious for days. If he hadn't found me I would have been dead in those bushes just as Caroline had planned. But he found me. He carried me as much as a mile to the safety of his cabin. Caroline had taken my clothes, I guess so no one would be able to recognize my body if it was found, or maybe to make it look like a sex crime or something. I'm not exactly sure. But…he…"

As she hesitated he realized she was still uncertain about revealing the man's identity. But Roy didn't push. The important thing right now was to get her story. He could get the details later.

"…he gave me his own shirt to wear," she continued. "He set my leg and splinted it. He gave me his bed and slept on the floor. He kept me alive, Daddy, and I guess it was touch and go for a while."

As she paused again she moved her leg down off his lap, knocking the pillow to the floor in the process and, placing both of her hands on his knees the way she used to do as a child when she begged him for something, let her eyes plead with him.

"Daddy, he didn't have to get involved," she continued. She was telling her story, but it was more like begging for understanding. "Caroline was the one who left me there to die. He could just have ignored what he saw. He could have left me there where Caroline put me and gone about his business. But he didn't, Daddy, he got involved. He saved my life. He nursed me back to health. He made huge sacrifices just to care for me. I owe him more than I can ever repay."

But? Roy wanted desperately to ask that question, but he didn't. He wanted to know just what sort of repayment this strange man had exacted from his little girl, but instead he asked, "Why didn't he just take you to a hospital?"

"He couldn't," she said, still leaning on his knees. "But before I tell you why you have to understand – he saved my life. I owe him for that. And he's a wonderful man – kind and generous, patient. He's a lot like you, Daddy, and I…I'll never forget him."

The sentiment of those words was echoed sharply in her eyes. There was no mistaking the deep feelings she had for this stranger, a man her father had never met, a man with whom she had spent three unchaperoned weeks in an isolated mountain cabin.

"Penny? What happened up there?" he asked as calmly as he could force himself to be.

"Nothing, Daddy," she assured him. "He was a perfect gentleman the whole time. He took care of me, he brought me flowers, and he slept on the floor."

"So why can't we tell anyone?" Roy asked. "If he was such a gentleman, so heroic, why not tell the world?"

Restlessly Penny got to her feet to stand staring out at the little chapel below. "Before I tell you that," she said, turning back to face him after a long, anxious minute, "you have to believe he's a wonderful person. He would never hurt anyone. He risked everything to help me, and I owe him my life."

Roy got to his feet to stand before her, taking her hands in his. "What is it, Penny? What is there about this man?"

Still she hesitated for a long moment. When she did finally speak it was with a strong hesitation in her voice, wanting to confide in him, yet still uncertain about doing so.

"He's...he was..."

As she stopped Roy saw in her eyes that her hesitation stemmed from a deep fear that he wouldn't accept her words for the truth, but the concern in his eyes finally brought the words forth in a plea for understanding.

"Two years ago his wife was murdered. They thought he did it. But he didn't. He couldn't have. He could never have hurt anyone. But they...they convicted him anyway. And if anyone found out about him he would be sent back to prison. I can't let that happen. I can't do that to him after he saved my life."

It was more than Roy could do to keep his surprise and concern from showing. "You're telling me this man is a convicted murderer? An escaped convict?"

"He didn't do it, Daddy, I know he didn't. It's just not in him to hurt anyone, never mind kill them."

"Penny, you don't know what people might do if provoked far enough..."

"No, Daddy, I spent time with him," she insisted. "If he had really killed someone do you think he would have any scruples against doing so again to protect his secret? But he didn't. Instead he saved my life after someone else tried to kill me. And when I discovered his secret he was scared to death that I would turn him in, but he was ready to run from the only safe home he'd had for the past year rather than hurt me in any way. In fact, he offered to carry me out of there first so I wouldn't be abandoned in the middle of nowhere with a broken leg. When he saw all of you out there he carried me up to meet you. Daddy, that's not the way a murderer would react. I know it."

There was no doubt as to her sincerity. She honestly believed in the man's innocence, but Roy had serious misgivings nonetheless. A young woman left for dead, not even remembering who she was, rescued by a man who knew how too use his charms, alone with that man for weeks... It was understandable that she might be confused into believing in an innocence that wasn't there.

"So, who is this man?" he asked, trying to keep his misgivings from showing, but she saw his doubts.

"You promised you wouldn't say anything," she reminded him with a deep note of concern in her voice.

"I know, Penny," he said. "But if the man is an escaped felon…"

"A wrongly convicted man who saved my life!" Penny insisted, impatiently moving away from him. "And prison would kill him. I can't let him be arrested. I won't let you turn him in. I gave him my word."

Roy sighed. "I won't say anything," he said. "But I think we should talk to him, convince him–"

"I won't ask him to turn himself in either," she insisted, frustrated that he wouldn't just accept her words for her hero's innocence. "And if you intend breaking your promise I will warn him so he can make his escape. I would even go with him into exile if necessary. And I would never trust you again."

Roy sighed again. This determination he was seeing in his daughter was unusual and seeing it now, seeing her desperation, increased his concern. He knew, however, that he had to watch his step here or she just might carry out her threat, going with an escaped felon into exile. He had to prevent that at all costs.

"Alright, Penny," he said. "If protecting this man's secret is so important, why tell me now?"

She came back to sit on her chair, waiting expectantly until he also returned to his seat.

"Because," she said with conviction. "I have to prove his innocence, and I can't do it alone."

The pleading in her eyes and in her voice was something he had never been able to deny her. From the time she was a tiny child it had always touched him to his very soul when she turned those sincere, imploring eyes pleading in his direction. Now was no exception, even if the whole idea of getting involved with a convicted criminal went against every thread of common sense.

"Please, Daddy," she begged, placing her hands on his knees again. "I've tried. I spent all day working on it, but I don't know what to do. If people see that I'm even interested they're going to wonder why. They'll know I must have personal reasons and they'll check to find out what they are. When they do they'll know where I must have met him, and they'll find him. I can't do that to him."

"Penny, I don't know that I can do any different," he said reluctantly.

"I know, if we even show an interest they're going to wonder why," she agreed with deep regret. "But I thought, maybe if we talked about it, we could come up with something…"

"Alright," he said without conviction. "Tell me about this young man of yours and we'll see what we can do."

With great relief and deep gratitude Penny kissed his cheek. Then, as thoroughly as she knew how, she told him the story of Michael Klotski. As she spoke, telling him everything that had happened to her from the time of waking up without any memory or concerns at all, to finding the clippings and Mike's subsequent explanation – including his reluctance to tell her any of it – to her own day's adventures in looking for answers, Roy spoke little, letting her tell her story in her own way, but when she finished, just sitting there waiting for his response, he knew she had convinced him that Michael Klotski was indeed an innocent man and that they had to do something to help him.

"I'm not sure I can do any better than you did," he said thoughtfully. He sat with his hands together in the form of a steeple, his chin set firm, his eyes staring at nothing. To Penny that was a good sign. He was thinking, trying to come up with a solution.

"What was the name of that club of his?" he asked finally.

"The Sunshine Health and Fitness Club," Penny said hopefully as she waited for whatever helpful suggestions he might offer.

Getting to his feet Roy moved over to the telephone, punched in a number, and a moment later asked if there was a listing for the Sunshine Health and Fitness Club. Apparently there was, and he wrote it down on the stationary pad provided by the hotel.

"Alright," he said, turning back to her. "I have an idea."

"You won't make them suspicious?" she begged.

"I'll be careful," he promised. "But I can't do it tonight, it's too late and I'm starved. What do you say we discuss it over dinner."

Due to the private nature of the subject they didn't actually discuss his idea until they were back in the suite after dinner. But then Penny was impatient and dying of curiosity.

"So what is this idea of yours?" she asked as they settled down on the sofa together.

"I'm not sure it will do any good," he said. "I can ask some questions without arousing any suspicions, but I don't foresee learning anything new. I'm sure his attorney has done all he could long ago. The two of us coming in here at this late date are not likely to help much."

"I know," Penny admitted unhappily. "But we have to try. It's not fair that a man like Mike has to spend the rest of his life on the run for something he didn't do."

Roy patted her leg with a sigh. "Alright, Honey," he said. "I'll do my best."

"So what are you going to do?" she asked.

"I thought I would go down to that club of his tomorrow," he said. "I can start by discussing the possibility of a discount program for our employees like we've done back home. This new contract to open up a branch here is a legitimate excuse for poking my nose into things, asking questions about the owner. They're not going to think anything about my wanting to know who I'm setting my employees up with."

The idea gave Penny hope. That would be a good excuse for asking questions. But concern for Mike kept her cautious.

"We'll have to be careful," she said. "If anyone was to get suspicious–"

"I'll be careful," he promised. "But you're going to have to wait for me here. It would look suspicious if I brought my daughter to a business meeting."

She knew he was right, but it was the hardest thing she could do the next morning to sit by and wait for the verdict – wanting to see for herself that no one was put on the alert about Mike, wishing desperately that she could be close enough to warn Mike if something went wrong.

Chapter Nine

For Roy's part, he had no difficulty keeping a business demeanor as he approached the club. At eight o'clock sharp he called and made an appointment to speak to the manager at one o'clock. He then took Penny for breakfast and some sightseeing to keep her mind off her worries until he had to leave for the club. As their flight home was scheduled for Wednesday morning, they had the rest of the day to do as they pleased, and he wanted to spend the time with his daughter, short as that was, before he left her at the hotel to see what he could do for her young man.

"I'm Roy Loftin," he told the young man who greeted him at the front desk. His name tag identified him as Craig. "I have an appointment to see Jack Stone."

"Yes, of course, Mr. Loftin," Craig said with a smile, his hand already on the phone. It was only a moment later that he had the manager on the line. "Mr. Stone, Mr. Loftin is here for his appointment… Yes, Sir."

He was already coming around the desk as he hung up. "Mr. Stone's office is right this way."

As he followed the young man through the lobby, down a short hall, past a pair of rest rooms, a drinking fountain, two closets marked 'linen' and 'equipment', Roy found he was impressed by the club's appearance. For a place where the owner had been absent for a year it seemed to be running remarkably well. In his mind that spoke well of the man to whom Penny had so obviously given her heart. It said he'd put the right people in charge from the beginning, and it said that despite all his difficulties the man was respected by those he'd left in charge. At least if it was still Michael Klotski's possession.

Not only did that leave Roy with the impression this Mike was a good businessman, but that he was a good man as well. Maybe he was being unduly influenced in his reasoning by the fact that Penny believed in the man so much, but his belief in her opinion was growing more and more solid all the time.

"Mr. Stone, Mr. Loftin," Craig introduced the two men, then left them alone, closing the door behind him.

"Thank you for seeing me on such short notice," Roy said in his perfect business tone. "As I mentioned on the phone my company is interested in working out a health incentive program for our employees. It's worked well for us in our head office and our other two branches, and now that we are opening up here in L.A. we are interested in starting a similar program here."

"Certainly, Mr. Loftin," Mr. Stone said. "We have arranged such programs for several local companies. How many employees are we talking about?"

For the next twenty minutes they discussed the details and the options in a friendly business fashion, as if that had been Roy's sole reason for being there. It was only when they had a basic plan in mind that Roy finally fitted his real purpose into the conversation as subtly as possible.

"My flight home is scheduled for eight A.M. tomorrow," he said. "Would it be possible to speak to the owner of the club before I leave?"

The expression on Mr. Stone's face did not change, but a guarded look, only half concealed, crept into his eyes.

"I'm sorry, Mr. Klotski is not available at the moment," he said. "But as the manager of the Sunshine Club I am authorized to make all necessary arrangements."

"I understand that, Mr. Stone," Roy said. "And I have nothing against doing my business with you. But I do have one concern."

He hesitated, as if choosing his words carefully, but in actuality he had thought them through thoroughly, rehearsing them in his mind a dozen times just since leaving the hotel.

"I understand that the owner, a…" he looked at his notes, "…Michael Klotski, has had some legal difficulties in the past."

The guarded look in Mr. Stone's eyes grew. "Mr. Klotski was…accused of a crime a couple of years ago," he admitted, clearly trying not to sound defensive. "But all charges have since been dropped. He has been completely vindicated. So I see no reason that any of that should affect our business."

"He's been completely vindicated?" Roy asked, trying not to look too shocked.

"Over six months ago," Mr. Stone assured him. "The real culprit was caught, confessed, and all charges against Mr. Klotski were subsequently dropped."

Roy felt a deep sense of relief sweep over him. If that was the case than there was nothing more that needed done. For Penny's sake he was grateful for the news.

"You'll pardon me for my concern," he said. "But I do have a responsibility toward my employees. I had heard your club is well-equipped and has a fine atmosphere. But I needed to be sure I was not recommending to my employees a club that would be having legal difficulties which would affect them. If, as you say, there are no problems in that area, I see no reason we cannot do business."

Mr. Stone relaxed, and they sat for several more minutes discussing and agreeing on the details of the contract Roy would sign with the club owned by Penny's friend who was still in hiding in the mountains without any awareness that his innocence had finally been proved.

Penny paced the floor of the main room of the suite heedless of her foot swelling in her cast. She could not sit still as she worried, so that, by the time she heard the key in the lock she was a nervous wreck.

"He's innocent," were the first words out of her father's mouth as he entered the room, before he had even closed the door, before she had a chance to even open her mouth with the question that had plagued her for an hour and a half. His very cheerfulness made her stop short in surprise.

"What?" she started. But he reached her side, took her by the hand, and drew her to the sofa.

"The case against him has been dropped," he said as he sat down, pulling her down beside him. "His sentence has been reversed. They've found the real killer. Your Mike is free."

"How do you know?" Penny demanded, wanting desperately to believe him, yet too cautious to accept the good news without reservation.

Her father told her of his conversation with Jack Stone, the manager, and his assurance that Michael Klotski had been freed of all accusation. But still Penny was wary.

"Are you sure?" she asked. "Maybe he was just telling you what you wanted to hear to get your business."

"Maybe," he said. "But I doubt it. He seemed sincere enough, and it would be too easy to check. Lying about it could get him into a lot of trouble, even fraud and misrepresentation. He wouldn't risk that."

"But we have to be sure," she insisted.

"We can check on it," he agreed. "What was the name of that judge who presided over his case?"

She had to look it up in her notes, then he called the courthouse for confirmation.

"It's true," he said as he hung up the phone. "The verdict was overturned on December nineteenth, more than six months ago."

Tears of relief filled Penny's eyes then. Mike was free at last. No longer did he have to hide from the world. He could go home, he could go anywhere he wanted without watching over his shoulder, without worrying that every person he saw was a danger to him – wanting to send him back to prison.

"We're not finished yet," Roy said, seeing her relief. "We know it's true, but is it likely this friend of yours is going to take our word for it? He's been running for a long time. If he's still afraid, he's going to need to see some proof before he reveals himself to the world again."

That was true. "So how do we get proof?"

"There's got to be court documents," he said. "Maybe we can get ourselves a copy."

"We still need to keep a low profile," Penny said. "If Mike wants publicity it should be his choice. It wouldn't be fair to have the world attack him for a story even before he's had a chance to learn the good news."

"Agreed," Roy said. "But that may not be so easy if we want copies of the court documents."

"Maybe his brother could help," she suggested. "If I could talk to him…according to Mike he was the only one to stand by him through the trial. Surely he would see the need for protecting Mike's privacy. And if he was to ask for a court document no one would connect Mike to me."

"It's worth a shot," Roy agreed.

It took a couple minutes for Penny to get Joseph Klotski's telephone number from information. Being just after three o'clock on a Tuesday afternoon there was a strong possibility that he would be working, but she was eager to try nonetheless.

"Hello?"

The voice that answered her ring was that of a woman, probably Mike's sister-in-law. The sounds of children playing could be heard in the background.

"May I please speak to Mr. Joseph Klotski?" Penny asked in her most professional tone.

"He's not in at the moment," the woman said. "This is Mrs. Klotski. Could I take a message?"

"Well, I…" Penny hesitated. "Is there another number where I could reach him? It's important that I reach him as soon as possible."

So that he has time to get me the proof I need before my flight in the morning, she added to herself.

"Well, if you would like to leave your name and number, I can try to reach him with a message to call you," Mrs. Klotski suggested.

"That's not possible," Penny said. "But it is urgent I speak with Mr. Klotski. It's…it's about his brother."

"Michael?" Mrs. Klotski's manner and voice changed instantly. "Do you know where he is? Is he okay?"

"I'd prefer discussing that with Mr. Klotski," Penny insisted. "Please, it's important. Is there a number where I can reach him right away?"

Mrs. Klotski immediately related a number which Penny wrote down on the note pad next to the phone. She then thanked her and, without hanging up, just touched the button to disconnect the call. As soon as she had a dial tone she began dialing the other number. So intent was she that she had completely forgotten her father's presence.

"Greyland Incorporated," a feminine voice said on the other end of the line after two rings. "May I help you?"

"Yes," Penny said. "May I please speak to Mr. Joseph Klotski?"

"May I tell him who is calling and the nature of your business?" the woman asked. Penny didn't like the tone of her voice, a tone that said, "You have to get past me first." But she was not about to be put off.

"You may tell him he doesn't know me, but that my business is urgent and involves him and his family personally," she said. She was determined to speak to the man, but she was not about to reveal any of her business, even her name, to anyone else.

For a moment the woman's pause made Penny feel she wasn't going to put her through and she was trying to decide what she would do about that when the woman spoke.

"Just a moment," she said, put out that Penny hadn't been more revealing as to the nature of her business. "I will see if he is available."

Penny was put on hold, fearing as she waited that she would not be put through at all, but a moment later a masculine voice, not unlike Mike's, answered.

"This is Joseph Klotski," he said. "To whom am I speaking?"

"I prefer not to give my name, Mr. Klotski," Penny said. "But I am calling about your brother, Mike."

"Mike!?"

There was an intense interest in his voice now, instant excitement, though controlled.

"You know Mike? Do you know where he is?"

"Mr. Klotski," she said, ignoring his questions. "I understand that the guilty verdict against Mike was overturned in December."

"Yes," he said. "Kurt Walker confessed. The judge pronounced Mike innocent and all charges were dropped. Does Mike know that?"

"Not yet…"

"Then you've got to tell him," Joe said. "You've got to let him know it's safe for him to come home."

"I've got to have some proof."

"I can get you proof," Joe said. "I can have it inside an hour. Just tell me where to bring it and I'll deliver it myself."

"I'm sure you'll agree, Mr. Klotski, that secrecy is important here," Penny said. "Mike has been through an awful lot these past two years, and the press has only made it worse. I think he deserves to hear this news privately, without the fanfare of the press, with some dignity and some pride. If you care about him at all you will keep this between us until I can show him the proof of his freedom. I'm sure he will get in touch with you then as soon as he can."

"I won't say a word," Joe promised. "But you've got to tell me where I can find him."

"Can I meet you some place in the next hour or two where we can discuss it?" she asked.

"I could meet you at my house in an hour," he said. "Twelve-forty-two, Bellefonte Drive."

"At your house?" she asked, looking for the first time to her father for his opinion. He shook his head. "Just a moment."

She covered the mouthpiece to keep Joe from overhearing and Roy whispered, "You don't know this man. Make it someplace public, the restaurant where we had lunch, maybe – the Hudson House."

With a nod she removed her hand from the mouthpiece to ask. "Can you meet me at the Hudson House Restaurant?"

"Certainly," he agreed. "Just as soon as I can get there. How will I know you?"

She covered the phone again. "How will we know each other?" she whispered to her father.

"Have him…have him remove his tie and jacket and lay them across the chair next to him," Roy said. "You'll find him."

"Are you wearing a suit jacket and tie?" Penny asked Joe.

"I am," he said. "Navy pinstripe, striped tie. Is Mike with you now?"

"If you will lay your jacket and tie over the back of the chair beside you I will find you," Penny said without answering his question. "I will meet you there in about an hour."

As she hung up the phone, before he could say anything else, her heart was pounding with nervous energy. All the cloak and dagger involved in protecting Mike's privacy was filling her with tension, yet the excitement of knowing he was free at last filled her with eager impatience to get it over with so that he could finally be rid of the lonely isolation that had been his life for so long.

As they waited for the next hour to pass, Penny and Roy discussed their plans. Roy insisted on going along to see that she was alright, but he agreed to stay out of sight unless he was needed. In fact, he would go in ahead of her and watch for Joe, watch to see that he was really alone before Penny approached him.

In accord with their plans, Roy was seated drinking coffee and eating a sandwich nearly ten minutes before the man in question came in. Even before Joe removed his coat and jacket it was clear to Roy who he was. The nervous excitement in him was clear to everyone in the restaurant that was only a quarter filled at four-fifteen.

As he moved to an empty table in the corner of the room, as far from the other diners as possible, a manila envelope in one hand, his eyes rapidly searched the room for the stranger he was to meet.

"Just coffee," he said in answer to the waitress' inquiry as he took a seat. He never let go of the envelope.

It was another five minutes before Penny came in, five minutes in which Joe sat in nervous anticipation, watching the door like a hawk when he was satisfied the woman he was to meet was not yet present.

As Penny entered through the front door he nearly got to his feet to meet her, but she ignored him completely and he stayed where he was, having decided she must not be the one he was to meet after all. When she took a seat at an empty table with her back to him, but where she could see her father's face, he turned back to watching the door.

Penny ordered the soup of the day, then glanced at her father as the waitress left her. His nod to go ahead was barely noticeable, but Penny knew it to mean he was convinced Joe was alone and that she should go ahead and meet him.

Nervously, her heart pounding violently in her chest, she got to her feet and walked back to Joe's table. The resemblance to Mike was so real that for a moment her heart flipped at the sight of him, and she knew she would have recognized him as Mike's brother in any crowd.

"Mr. Klotski," she asked as she took a seat across the table from him.

"You're the woman who knows Mike?" he asked in a hoarse whisper, startled to find that she was the person he was looking for after all.

"I am," she said. "Do you have the proof we discussed?"

"Right here," he said, quickly passing the envelope to her. "Where is he? Is he okay?"

"He's fine," she said. "Physically, anyway. Emotionally he's been through more than he deserves. He feels totally betrayed – first by his wife and her lover, then by the justice system in convicting him of a crime he didn't commit, and lastly by the people closest to him who didn't believe in his innocence."

Joe looked ashamed. "I wanted to believe him," he said. "But the evidence seemed so…he was standing over the body, it was his gun…"

The arrival of the waitress with Penny's order interrupted him. "Do you wish to have your meal served here, Ma'am, or at your own table?"

"Here, please," Penny said, aware of the woman's curiosity about the strange way she had changed tables, but not about to satisfy it.

"I'm not here to judge you, Mr. Klotski," she continued in a quiet tone as soon as the waitress was gone. "I'm only here to help Mike."

"I just want to help him, too," Joe assured her as she took a bite of her soup, then added as she turned her attention to the envelope he had given her. "That's a certified court document, signed by Judge Lincoln. The others are just a couple news clippings I saved. You'll give them to him as soon as possible?"

"I will," she promised. "It may be two or three days before I see him, but I will give them to him as soon as I can."

As she spoke, her eyes were on the court paper she had slipped from the envelope. The Judge's signature, the court seal…

Suddenly an open napkin came down over the paper, effectively covering it from her view, and she looked up at Joe in surprise as to why he would do that. But his reason was immediately clear as the curious waitress approached the table.

"More coffee, Sir?" the woman asked, her curiosity only increased by the secrecy they displayed in covering up the papers.

Joe nodded his assent to the coffee, remarking as she filled the cup, "That will be all for now. We'll let you know if we need anything else."

The waitress looked put out by the dismissal, but she moved away and Penny put the paper and the clippings back into the envelope. She could read them later when there was no audience.

"Do you mind if I ask you something?" he asked as she turned her attention back to her soup.

"I make no promise to answer," she said with a soft smile. "But you're welcome to ask."

"How do you happen to know Mike?"

Penny hesitated before answering. Even though she knew that Joe's only interest was a concern for the brother he hadn't seen in a year, Penny didn't want to embarrass Mike by telling his brother anything that had happened between them. If Mike wanted Joe to know he could tell him the whole story later.

"It's a long story," she said finally, not taking her eyes off her soup.

"But you're in love with him."

Her eyes snapped to his at the positive tone of his words. How could he know that? How could she let him think such a thing? What if he told Mike? What if Mike didn't feel the same? What if her feelings were an embarrassment to him? She couldn't do that to him, nor could she take a chance that her feelings might in some way make Mike feel obligated to her after her help in getting proof of his innocence. If there was ever to be anything between them it had to be based on mutual feelings, not on obligation.

"My feelings for your brother are my business, Mr. Klotski," she said impatiently as she abandoned the rest of her soup and got to her feet. "And I should be going."

Before she could take a step away, though, he also was on his feet. "Wait, please," he said, standing in her path. "Please, I'm sorry. You're right. It's none of my business. But please, you've got to let me know how to get in touch with him. If I could just talk to him–"

"I'll inform Mike of your request as soon as I see him," she promised. "If you will excuse me–"

"Wait! Please! Miss...please, he's my brother."

The pleading in his voice and in his eyes softened her indignation toward him. He was worried. He hadn't meant to pry. He hadn't meant to embarrass her. He wanted only to know that his brother was alright.

Her whole countenance softened with her voice as she said, "He's okay, Mr. Klotski. And I'm sure he will want to see you as soon as he knows it is safe to do so. It will be a couple of days before I can see him, but you should hear from him by the weekend."

"Thank you," he said with deep gratitude. "And wait. Give him this, too."

Reaching into his pocket he pulled out two plastic cards.

"These are his driver's license and his ATM card," he explained. "He may need some money or something. The card is still active. And let me give you my home phone number so you can call me day or night if there is anything–"

"I have your number," Penny interrupted. "Your wife was the one who gave me your office number."

"Great," he said. "Call me if there is anything I can do. And, please, tell Mike I am so sorry for doubting him. And tell him also everything is waiting for him – his house, his club, his brother–"

"I'll tell him," Penny promised. "And you will hear from him by the weekend I'm sure. But now I really should be going."

He thanked her again as he let her pass, and followed her to the cash register near the door.

"Let me get that," he said as the waitress handed them each a check slip.

"That's not necessary, Mr. Klotski," she said firmly, and he didn't argue as she paid her bill and walked out.

From the moment she walked out of the restaurant after her meeting with Joe, Penny could think of nothing but getting back to Mike with the good news of his vindication. It was the subject of her thoughts every waking moment, the theme of her dreams while she slept, the substance of every conversation she shared with her father so long as no one was around to overhear.

In their conversations she and her father worked up an entire plan of action which she started putting into motion the minute she returned to her apartment on Wednesday evening. One of her first tasks was to call Joe again.

"Is Mr. Klotski there?" she asked as it was again answered by his wife.

"Yes, of course," she said immediately. "Is this the woman who called about Michael?"

Penny didn't have to answer. Her husband immediately took the phone. He sounded as if he was still chewing and, as it was eight o'clock in the Ozarks, it would be six in Los Angeles. She realized she must have caught him in the middle of his dinner, though he didn't seem to mind in the least.

"This is Joe," he said. "Is Mike with you?"

"Not at the moment," Penny said. "I haven't even had a chance to see him yet, but I was thinking – is it possible for you to travel by Friday?"

"I can arrange it," he agreed without argument. "Where should I meet you?"

"Can you be in Tulsa, Oklahoma by six p.m. central time?" she asked.

"Is that where Mike is?"

"I expect him to be there by then," she said. "When you get to Tulsa, take a cab to the Golden Sun Restaurant on sixteenth."

"I'll be there," he promised. "Will Mike be there?"

"I haven't seen him yet, Mr. Klotski," she said. "So I can make no promises. But if he knows you're going to be there I am sure he will be."

"I'll be there," he promised again. "And thank you."

There were several other arrangements to make before Penny called it a day – telephone calls and shopping among them – so it was nearly midnight before she got to bed. Even so, anticipation and excitement about what lay ahead filled her thoughts and her dreams long after her head hit the pillow.

The anxiety Penny felt as her father helped her into the saddle the next morning was stronger than any she had ever felt before. How would Mike react to seeing her again? Would he give her a chance to tell him the news? Or would fear of her motives send him into hiding before she had a chance even to speak to him? Was he even still out here? Or had he moved on as soon as she was gone so that she could not expose him to anyone?

It was early, not yet seven-thirty, but it was not the early morning chill that made her shiver. It was the uncertainty of what lay ahead. Roy did not miss her apprehension.

"Are you sure this is what you want to do?" he asked as he adjusted the stirrups for her.

"I have to tell him, Daddy," she said.

"But are you sure you want to do it this way?" he asked. "Are you sure you want me to just leave you here?"

She gave him a smile of reassurance. "I'll be fine," she promised. "I was out here for three weeks and I wasn't even prepared. This time I have food, clothing, a sleeping bag, a flashlight, and transportation on ol' Star here. I'll be fine overnight, I promise."

Roy stood stroking Star's neck for a moment, another concern obviously on his mind.

"What is it, Daddy?" she asked. "Is it the idea of me spending the night alone with Mike in that cabin? I did so for three weeks, you know, and I'm still as pure as you raised me to be."

"I trust you," he said absently. Apparently that wasn't his concern.

"Then what's bothering you?" she asked, reaching down to touch her father's hand as it rested on Star's neck.

He turned serious eyes in her direction, cupping her hand in both of his. "I know how you feel about this guy, Penny," he said. "And I know you're hoping that once he knows about the changed verdict he'll want to be with you. But you can't count on that."

Penny bit her lip and swallowed the pain that thought brought her. She did want Mike to want her. She prayed for that. But she knew her father was right. She couldn't count on it.

"I don't want you to be hurt," he added. "He's been alone out there for a long time. And he was hurt and betrayed by everyone he felt close to, most especially his wife. He may find it difficult to give his heart a second time."

"I know, Daddy," she said with a sigh. "I have thought of that. But I…he saved my life. Whatever the outcome, I owe him this."

She bent to kiss his forehead, then twisted the reins, pressed her knees into Star's sides to start her moving, and started off to give good news to the one man she loved with all her heart.

Chapter Ten

The sound of a motor vehicle starting up caught Mike's attention as he reached the end of his trap line. Instantly alert he moved to the edge of the trees to find the source of the sound — just in time to see a mini-van with a horse trailer on behind pull away from the turnout at the top of the bluff across the river. Recognizing it as the same one in which Penny had ridden away only a week and a half ago he felt suddenly tense, immediately cautious.

Why was it here? Had someone been dropped off here? Was it Penny? Or had someone come in search of him? He could see no one, but that could be because they were already on the path down the hill. They could even be across the river and on their way up this side by now.

Panic filled him. Whether anyone was out there or not there had to have been a reason for that van to have stopped there, to have returned to the scene of Penny's attack. Could it be an attempt to uncover evidence against that woman – Caroline? Or was it…?

And then he saw her – Penny – riding a roan mare down to the water's edge. Pain hit him like a knife through his heart. What was she doing here? Obviously the person in the van had dropped her off. But why? And was she alone?

It didn't matter. Clearly she had betrayed him. Even if she was by herself, no one would have dropped her off out here all alone unless she had told them about him. She had betrayed him. Why had he ever believed her? Why had he allowed himself to think of her non-stop since she'd gone? To dream of her? To see her smiling at him from his bed in the mornings? To see those beautiful legs of hers beneath the tail of his shirt? To hear her sweet, musical voice humming softly as she had done so often?

But she had betrayed him. Whatever her reason for being here, whatever her motive, he had trusted her with the most important secret of his life, and she had not kept it. Now he was going to have to pack up his things and move on, and hope he did not leave enough of a back trail to be followed.

The roan came up over the rise and he kept under cover as he watched her move off in the direction of his trap line. So far there was no sign of anyone else across the river. So apparently she was alone. But why? What was she doing here? And just how much had she told others about him?

At least she hadn't brought the police with her, he thought as he followed quietly behind her, being careful not to let her know he was there. That was some consolation. And he could see she was carrying full saddle bags. Did she think she was helping him by bringing him supplies? That would be just like her. He'd saved her life, so she was grateful. It was completely in keeping with the spirit of kindness and compassion he had seen in her to want to repay him in such a way.

But didn't she know what she was doing to him by coming here? Didn't she know that just by returning here she was making a trail for others to follow? He doubted she would purposely hurt him, but her good intentions could ruin him.

Halfway through a small clearing she stopped, and from the way she sat studying her surroundings, he had a feeling she was trying to get her bearings. The only time she had been though here conscious was when he had carried her through to meet her family. She was having difficulty remembering which way to go, and for a moment he contemplated leaving her to her own devises, letting her get lost. It would serve her right for butting in, for coming back here where she didn't belong, where she wasn't wanted, putting him in jeopardy.

But if she was lost, then the person who had left her here would come looking for her, probably bringing others with him, and that would only serve to make matters worse. So, when she started off in the wrong direction he felt he had to do something, though he was not going to treat her with kid gloves no matter what her motive in coming back.

"What are you doing here?" he demanded harshly from behind her.

Startled, Penny reined in the mare and pulled her around to face him. The smile on her face at seeing him was one of real delight, but Mike was not about to be taken in by that. She had betrayed him, just like that rest of the world. That was all he could allow himself to think about now.

"What are you doing here?" he demanded again.

The smile left her face. Perhaps she had expected him to be pleased to see her. But he was not pleased. He was angry and he was upset that his trust in Penny had been as misplaced as his trust in Diane had been. Women were all alike. People were all alike. None of them could be trusted when the chips were down. And after he had saved her life. He had been so sure that act alone had left her grateful enough to keep his secret. But it hadn't, and the pain of that betrayal ran deep.

"I came to bring you…" she started, but he interrupted her.

"I don't need anything from you!" he snapped at her. "I thought I had something once – your word. But obviously that means nothing to you. Now all I want is for you to go back where you came from. Get out of my life!"

"I haven't broken my word to you, Mike," she said, her voice calm even in the face of his anger. "I told you—"

"You told me you wouldn't tell anyone about me," he insisted sarcastically. "So how long did it take them to torture it out of you?"

The look in her face at his angry outburst was one of pity or possibly sufferance for the attitude she saw in him that she didn't like but did understand. But it only made him more upset. He didn't need pity, least of all from a woman who was willing to break her word and then lie to him about it.

"I didn't–"

"How dare you?" he interrupted. "How dare you lie to me? Do you honestly expect me to believe you told no one about me? That they brought you out here and left you without even asking any questions? I know better than that. No one who loved you would leave you here alone without an explanation. Neither would anyone else. You had to have told them – against your word!"

"I believe what I promised, Mike," she said calmly, "was that I would not do or say anything that would get you sent back to prison. I have kept my word on that."

"Then you're a stupid fool if you think you haven't made anyone suspicious," he said. "You've left a trail a child could follow."

For the first time her face grew hard at his calling her a stupid fool. "I'm not a fool, Mike," she said in a serious tone so low as to be barely audible. "When you're ready to hear my explanation let me know."

"I don't need explanations, you idiot. I only need–"

But she was no longer paying any attention. Instead she had turned the mare back around and was riding away.

"Where are you going?" he demanded. If she thought she was leaving as he hoped she was, she was going in the wrong direction. If she thought she was going to the cabin, that, too, was the wrong way.

"I'm going to the cabin to make breakfast," she said, stopping to face him again. "And then…"

"I don't need you waiting on me either," he snapped.

But she continued speaking as if she hadn't heard him. "…when you're ready to shut up long enough to hear what I've done and the good news I came to bring you, I will be perfectly willing to discuss it with you."

With that she turned in the wrong direction and urged her horse onward.

"Fine, get yourself lost," he murmured as she went. Then he turned in frustration and walked toward the cabin on his own.

Not having heard his comment about getting lost, Penny continued off in the wrong direction for about a hundred feet. As she went, though unaware that she was taking a wrong path, she was aware that Mike was going off in another direction and, as upset as he was, as fearful of being caught and returned to prison as she knew him to be, she feared he would leave the area right then without ever learning of the overturned verdict.

In an effort to prevent that from happening she turned once again and went in search of him, catching up to him at the top of a knoll where she could see the smoke from the cabin chimney in the distance. So, he was going to the cabin after all, and she'd been going in the wrong direction. Of course he could still have been planning to pack up his things and leave, something she could not allow him to do without an explanation.

"Mike–"

"Go away!"

He didn't even turn as she came up behind him, but continued on in frustrated determination.

"Would you like a ride?" she asked.

He just ignored her.

Silence. That was good. Maybe she could tell him the good news at last.

"I thought you would like to know–"

"Haven't you messed up my life enough?!" he demanded, rounding on her in anger. "I saved your life! I took care of you! I gave you the shirt off my back, for crying out loud! And how do you repay me? By going against the one thing I asked you to do, the one thing you promised to do. Well, don't expect me to thank you. And don't expect me to stick around while you finish me off for good."

He whipped around again to continue his decent to the cabin – still only visible by the smoke descending from it's chimney. The full extent of his feelings were evident in his tone, in his eyes, and in the determined pace of his stride. His pain at the thought that she had betrayed him stabbed at her heart as nothing ever had before. His wife had betrayed him. He'd felt betrayed and abandoned by everyone he knew at the time of his trial when they had not believed in him. Even the justice system had let him down. And now he felt she had betrayed him as well. He was used to being betrayed. He expected it. But that didn't make it hurt any less.

For a moment she sat still on Star's back just watching him walk. His very stride and the slope of his shoulders cried out with his pain. Somehow she had to get through that anger and that pain that had him interrupting her every time she opened her mouth.

He walked on another hundred fifty feet while she removed the envelope of papers from the saddle bag, but on horseback it didn't take her long to catch up. He didn't look at her as she rode up alongside him, but the glare on his face made her decide that many more attempts to break through this present mood of his with conversation may take him beyond the breaking point.

"Read this," was all she said as she held out the envelope to him. But he didn't take it. Just walked on by, ignoring her completely.

Well, she could be just as stubborn, Penny decided. She rode up to a point about ten feet in front of him and dropped the envelope to the ground.

"Don't do something you'll regret," she said. Then she rode on ahead without looking back.

Why couldn't that woman leave him alone? Mike asked himself as he glared after her. Why did she have to be so insanely stubborn? Whatever was in that envelope he was inclined to leave it where it lay. It would serve her right if he did, or better yet, he could rip it to pieces and throw it in her face. Maybe then she would get the message and leave him in peace.

With that in mind he walked ahead and retrieved it from the ground where she had dropped it. But her words halted him before he ripped it. "Don't do something you'll regret." She expected him to regret it if he didn't at least look at what was in that envelope.

So, fine. He could look. He would look just to see what she thought was so important she had to break her words to him. It wasn't sealed. He could just as easily put it back into the envelope and rip it up later. He could take a quick look at it and still throw it in her face.

As the news clippings had all fallen to the bottom of the envelope, the only thing he saw upon opening it was the full-sized document. When his first quick glance showed him the court seal and the judge's signature, thoughts of the trial and conviction flashed into his mind, visions of prison that had for so long tormented his worst nightmares preventing him from seeing the rest of the document for a long moment.

Then suddenly one word jumped out at him as if it was the only word on the page. "Innocent." Suddenly every word on that page was more important than breathing.

"Judgment against Michael James Klotski...verdict overturned...declared innocent...released from all..."

He was dreaming. He read it again.

"...verdict overturned..."

He sank to his knees, unable to take his eyes from the page, yet unable to believe what he was reading.

"...innocent of all charges..."

He sank to the ground. Tears filled his eyes. And he read it again.

"...declared innocent..."

The tears fell. He was free. It was over at last. All this time. The pain, the humiliation, the hiding and fearing, the loneliness. It was over. He, Michael James Klotski, was at long last a free man.

And yet it was all so unreal, a dream that he could not fully believe. Too much time had passed, too much time in which fear and uncertainty had been the major motivating forces in his life, affecting everything he did, everything he thought. It was hard to let that go so suddenly.

But the proof was right there before him in black and white, with the judge's signature and the court seal to authenticate it. It was real. It was true. As unbelievable as it was, it was true. He was free at last. Penny had brought his proof that he was free at last.

Penny. He looked up in the direction she had gone, but she was now out of his sight. She may even have reached the cabin by now since she was on horseback.

Penny. She had brought this to him. She had come all this way to give him the proof of his freedom, and he had attacked her instead of listening.

Penny. All the things he had accused her of – betrayal. She'd tried to explain, but he'd refused even to let her speak. He'd yelled at her, flung accusations at her, refused even to give her the benefit of the doubt.

Penny. Sweet, beautiful, gentle, wonderful Penny. How could he have treated her so harshly? How could he have suspected her of anything but the most generous motives? How could he ever face her again after accusing her so unjustly? How could she ever forgive his unreasonableness?

Feeling a strange combination of emotions – guilt and regret for his mistreatment of the most wonderful woman in the world, the bearer of the best news he had ever received in his life, yet utter relief that at last he was a free man – he reread the court document yet again.

Free at last. Free to rejoin the world. Free to take back his life, the life that had so wrongly been denied him so long ago.

But was that the life he wanted now? How would he be received at home? At his club? In the world he had run from so long ago? Granted he now had a release from his conviction, the judge had declared him innocent, but would that be enough for the people who had doubted him so long ago? Would they now believe in his innocence? Or would they think it was just a technicality? Would they continue to resent and distrust him?

The paper didn't give reasons for the changed verdict. It only stated the fact. So what had changed the judge's mind? According to the date on the paper it had been signed six months ago. Had they discovered new evidence? Had the guilty party been caught? Or was it only some legal technicality that his attorney had at last discovered?

He had no answers. But he knew that Penny probably did, though after his harsh accusations he wouldn't blame her if she refused to give them to him. But he had to try. If he had to grovel at her feet for forgiveness he would do so. He would never doubt her again.

After one last look at the most important paper he had ever seen in his life, he opened the envelope to slide it back in for safe keeping. But it didn't want to go. A quick look inside showed that it was catching on some small newspaper clippings and he quickly upended the envelope to dump them out into his hand. There were two of them.

"*New evidence in O'Clair murder*," was the headline of a very short article.

"On June twenty-second of this year a jury of his peers found Michael Klotski guilty of the first degree murder of his wife, Diane O'Clair. Throughout the trial Klotski insisted on his innocence, but it is only now, thanks to the efforts of Klotski's attorney, Clyde Young, and Klotski's brother, Joseph Klotski, that there is evidence to support his claims.

"What that evidence is, which is now in the hands of the police and Judge Howard Lincoln, has thus far been withheld from the press, but according to Detective Lloyd Baskins, a new arrest is expected within the next twelve hours."

New evidence? A new arrest? Then it wasn't a technicality. Evidence. Another arrest. But who, and how? He quickly turned to the other clippings for an answer.

"Ford Confesses in O'Clair Murder. Previous Verdict Overturned." said another article.

"Due to the efforts of attorney, Clyde Young, and of Joseph Klotski, brother of the man previously convicted of the murder of Diane O'Clair, new evidence has prompted Brian Ford to confess to that murder himself.

"Ford, a neighbor of Klotski's who testified against him during the trial, has now confessed to having had an affair with the deceased extending over a period of eight months. When O'Clair informed him she was ending the affair because of her affair with another man, Steve Duncan, their angry confrontation ended with her death.

"Having only that morning removed her husband's gun from the locked cabinet where he kept it at his club, Ford claims she had threatened him with it if he didn't leave her alone and it went off twice as he tried to take it from her it. As he heard Klotski entering through the back door he panicked and made his escape through the front door. It was only as he became aware of another neighbor running toward the house at the sound of the shot that he returned, pretending also to have heard the shot, thus putting himself in the clear and adding further damaging testimony to Klotski's case.

"When confronted with the evidence of the time element involved which proved that his story could not have been true, Ford confessed, prompting Judge Lincoln to overturn the verdict against Klotski. Klotski incidentally has not been seen since an escape attempt by a fellow prisoner released him the day after the verdict against him was handed down and thus has not been informed of the changed judgment."

Brian Ford had killed Diane? The man had never seemed to like Mike, always avoiding him when possible, speaking only the few words that were deemed necessary for politeness' sake when they did meet. But Mike had never suspected the man of having had an affair with Diane. Had Diane been playing around with every man she knew? Were Steve Duncan and Brian Ford the only ones? How could he have been so blind to her activities for so long?

Yet, looking back, he could see how it was possible. She'd always craved attention. She'd often flirted with other men right in front of him. Yet he had excused her. She was only being friendly. He'd believed her to be faithful to him because he'd wanted to believe it.

But she'd always needed attention as much as she'd needed water or air. As she aged and her modeling jobs became fewer and less prestigious, he could see how she might look elsewhere for the adulation she was losing in her career. And his days had always been busy at his club. He hadn't been there throughout the days, day after day leaving her alone when she needed him. He'd been working, giving her only his evenings and as much time as he could on weekends, so she had found her attention elsewhere.

But Brian Ford? The man had always been so aloof, so withdrawn and unfriendly, at least to Mike. Was that only because he was having an affair with Mike's wife? Apparently so.

The fact that his story had not held up under scrutiny made sense to Mike now that he thought about it. His house was quite a distance from Mike's, twice as far as Luke Roberts' house. Yet they had arrived at the same time. If Mike had not been so badly in shock at the time maybe he would have thought of that then.

But he hadn't, no one had before or during the trial. But thanks to Joe and Clyde Young the truth had been told at last. Mike was free. And thanks to Penny he knew it. He should have been grateful to her for making this effort for him, to relieve him of the fear, the need to hide from the world. But instead he had yelled at her, had flung accusations at her.

Carefully he slipped the clippings and the court paper back into the envelope and got to his feet. It was time to face her, to confess his stupidity and to beg her forgiveness with all the humility he possessed.

The mare was tethered loosely to a small tree in a grassy patch a few feet from the cabin as Mike approached – the saddle and saddlebags still on her back as she grazed without a care. If only he could relax as easily.

Apparently Penny had planned to stay. There was a sleeping bag tied behind the saddle. But she must have changed her mind after his unreasonable response to her arrival because saddle bags and sleeping bag were both still in place.

Knowing he had no right to expect otherwise only made him feel more guilty than ever, but he drew up the courage to open the door nonetheless. Unexpected smells met him – bacon, pancakes, coffee – made him momentarily forget everything else. He hadn't even smelled such things in so long he had forgotten what they smelled like.

Penny stood at the stove, a camp coffee percolator on the back burner, a flat griddle across the front with a pancake frying on one side, several slices of bacon on the other. Just a brief glance at him as he came through the door was all the acknowledgment she gave him. He didn't blame her for ignoring him after his rough treatment of her earlier, but it was going to make his apology that much harder.

Slowly he came in, hesitating to approach her as he deliberated his words. Should he just confess his stupidity, or should he get down on his knees and beg her forgiveness the way she deserved?

"Sit down," she said as she removed the pancake from the grill to a plate and topped it with half a dozen slices of crisp bacon. "Would you like coffee?" she added as she set the plate down on the table next to the knife and fork she had already placed there. In the center of the table there was also a cube of butter and a bottle of syrup for his pancake, as well as a small cup of sugar cubes and a little plastic jar of what he assumed was powdered creamer for the coffee.

"You didn't have to do this, Penny," he said, the guilt growing in him.

First she'd come out here in a cast, on horseback, to bring him the greatest news of his life. Then she'd had to endure his unreasonable wrath and unfounded accusations, and now she was waiting on him with the best breakfast he'd ever smelled.

"I most certainly did," she denied firmly. But then she met his eyes and she smiled. "Sit down," she repeated in that sweet, kind voice that had haunted him every moment since she'd gone from him. "We can discuss it over breakfast."

"I'm sorry, Penny," he said in sincere apology. "You came here to help me and I turned on you like a wild man. I am so sorry."

"No need to apologize," she said as she took him by the hand to lead him the few steps to the chair and his waiting breakfast. "I understand completely. I even half expected it. But it's over. It's forgotten. So eat your breakfast and then I'll tell you everything I've done."

Only when he took the seat she offered did she return to the stove to pour more pancake batter on the griddle and remove the rest of the bacon to a second plate. She then poured two cups of coffee which she brought to the table while she let the second pancake cook.

"Eat," she commanded cheerfully as he sat watching her. So he ate, and the food tasted better than any he had ever tasted.

As she sat down across from him a few minutes later, though, he spoke again. "Penny, I…I am sorry. I should have listened…"

"It's forgotten," she said cheerfully. "And I do understand. I know how it looked, and the fact that you were feeling…betrayed…is also natural under the circumstances. I won't hold it against you, I promise. In return I hope you will forgive me for not completely keeping my word."

His laugh was self-mocking. "I can hardly complain considering what you've done for me. I thought I'd spend the rest of my life as a fugitive…"

As his voice trailed off Penny confessed, "All the same, I did break my word. I promised not to get you sent back to prison, and if you hadn't already been vindicated I might easily have done just that."

She told him all she had done, leaving nothing out of her account up to her meeting with Joe, confessing her nearly disastrous efforts to find answers. But rather than being upset with her as before, he felt only extreme gratitude. Maybe she had taken risks he would have found too dangerous, but she'd done it with the greatest of motives, and she had gone out of her way to keep her mistakes from hurting him.

"Thank you, Penny," he said when she was finished. "There's no way I can repay you for this, but I…"

"I didn't do anything," she said. "Your brother and your attorney did that."

"But I would never have known about it without you," he insisted. "I would have been out here…forever…never knowing I could leave."

"Being a messenger is easy," she replied with a smile.

As her story was so detailed they were both long since finished eating, and now she got to her feet to clear the table and begin washing the dishes.

"It was more than that, Penny," he insisted as he got to his feet to assist her with the washing up. "You gave me back my life. You don't know how that feels."

"And you don't know how it feels to know you saved my life," she said seriously, meeting his eyes. "So I guess that makes us even."

A strong craving to pull her into his arms hit him just then as she stood looking up into his face. But he resisted the impulse. She was grateful to him for saving her life, and she had repaid him for that debt. There was no indication she felt anything more for him than that.

"I guess it does," he said quietly instead. And they washed the few dirty dishes together in silence.

"So what are your plans now that you're free?" she asked as they finished a few minutes later. "Will you be going back to Los Angeles…and your club and everything?"

Something in her voice just then made him look at her. Could it be that she would be sorry to see him go? But she wasn't even looking at him as she turned to wipe down the table.

"I don't know," he said, watching her. "I haven't really thought about it."

"No, I suppose not," she agreed.

With the dishes done and the water emptied, Penny turned to Mike. "Is there anything you have to do just now?" she asked.

"Nothing in particular, I suppose," he said.

"Then can we sit down?" she asked. "There's some things I would like to discuss with you."

"Yes, of course," he agreed. Anything she wanted was agreeable to him just then. "But…do you mind if I ask you something?"

"Ask away," she said pleasantly as she again took a seat at the table.

He hesitated just briefly. "How long do you…intend to stay?"

Her frown indicated she thought he couldn't wait to be rid of her and, as that was the furthest thing from his mind, he quickly explained.

"I only ask because I noticed your mare is loaded down. I just thought if you intended to stay a while maybe we should unsaddle her before too long."

"My father won't be back to get me until noon tomorrow," she said. As she waited for his response to that – to see if he minded her staying that long – he gave her a smile of welcome that came up from his heart. He did want her to stay, for just as long as she was willing to stay, but he could never pressure her to do so, so it was a relief to know she wanted to be there.

"Then maybe we should unpack your things first," he said.

Agreeable to his suggestion, she followed him outside where he removed the saddle, saddle bags, blanket, and sleeping bag – leaving only the harness in place with which to keep the mare from wandering off. Carrying both the saddle and the saddle bags, he left only the blanket and sleeping bag for Penny to carry as they returned to the cabin. The saddle he placed in a corner of the room where it would be out of the way. The saddle bags he placed on the bed so she would have easy access to her belongings.

"So, what would you like to talk about?" he asked as he took a seat at the table.

Now that he was ready to talk she seemed to hesitate. He watched as she moved to sit on the bed, leaning back against the wall behind while she propped her foot up on the roll of the sleeping bag.

"I thought I should finish telling you all I've done," she said as he waited.

"Besides bringing me knowledge of my freedom?" he asked with a smile. He was feeling good just now – free from the fear of imprisonment, with Penny's forgiveness and her company to make him feel warm all over. It seemed another lifetime since he'd last felt this good.

"I told you I spoke to your brother, Joe," she said. "That he was the one who gave me the court paper and the news clippings."

Mike frowned. "There's nothing wrong with Joe? Or Karen and the kids?"

"No, no, well nothing except that he's worried about you," she assured him. "Really worried. So I…I arranged for him to fly out here tomorrow to meet you."

"Joe is coming here?"

"Well, not here," she amended. "Not to the cabin. But he's coming to Tulsa to meet you tomorrow night if you want to see him."

"Joe is coming all the way from California?" It seemed incredible.

"He's been worried about you," she said. "He's done a lot for you – much more than I did. And he is sorry for doubting you. I really think you should meet him."

She was pleading and he gave her a smile. "I want to see him," he promised. "He's my brother, the only family I have. And he stood by me when no one else did. I just can't believe he's coming all this way."

Her relief was clear. "A friend of my father's owns a restaurant in Tulsa," she said. "We've arranged for you to meet Joe there. Oh, and he sent you these."

From the pocket of her shirt she retrieved the driver's license and the ATM card.

"He thought you might need these," she said as she got up to hand them to him. "In case you need anything before he sees you, or before you get home."

Staring at the face that looked up at him from the license filled him with strange feelings. In another month and a half that license would expire, and it was as if a whole life time had come and gone since it was first issued.

"There's another thing," she said after returning to her seat on the bed.

He looked over at her, but she was not looking at him now, which immediately made him curious and concerned. He knew her well enough now to know that this look on her face meant that whatever she had to say was making her feel nervous and uncertain – probably about his reaction. She did say it, though, before he spoke.

"Daddy and I thought, with everything that's happened, you may prefer not to return home just yet. And if not, Daddy has an opening in his office for an assistant manager if you want the job."

A strange feeling gripped him. "Your father…would give me a job? He doesn't even know me."

"He knows you saved my life," she said. "He trusts you. And he knows you made a success of your own business before all this happened. You have experience. Those are qualities he's looking for."

Mike got to his feet to stand looking out through the window. So much was happening so quickly. Two years ago his whole life had been turned upside down overnight. He'd lost Diane, he'd lost his freedom, he'd lost the confidence and trust of his brother and his friends. Now suddenly everything was changing again. He was free at last. The blight against him was gone. And now Penny's father, a man he'd never met, was willing to entrust him with an important position in his company.

That of course was Penny's doing. She had, no doubt, influenced her father because of her own gratitude to him for rescuing him. But he could not repress the glorious feelings that filled him at once again being trusted.

"Of course you don't have to decide right now," Penny said as he remained silent. "It's just to give you an option."

Turning from the window he glanced over at her, trying to decide how she felt about that. Now that she had repaid him for her life by giving him back his own, would she be glad to see him go out of her life forever? Or was there even the remotest chance that she might wish for him to stay? But he could not be certain from her face.

"So," she said as she met his eyes. "Daddy will be picking me up at noon tomorrow. You're welcome to come with us. We can take you to meet Joe in Tulsa."

"Then I guess I'd better take care of a couple things," he said. "Starting by springing my traps."

He moved to the door, and Penny let him go without another word. And he couldn't help wondering just what she thought of him now that she had given him back his life, now that she had no reason to feel indebted to him for saving her life.

Chapter Eleven

Mike's nerves were strung as tight as guitar strings as he and Penny climbed the hill toward the road where her father was already waiting. Despite his attempts to hide his feelings, Penny was not fooled, and she understood completely how he was feeling. Not only was he about to meet the father of the woman with whom he had spent three unchaperoned weeks, not knowing how that man was going feel about him, but he was preparing to meet the life he had given up so long ago.

For two years now he had been an outcast – accused and unwanted by the people he had been closest to, isolated for one of those years with only his own thoughts and memories to keep him company. Now he was going back to that world, uncertain how he would be received by those same people, with only a court document giving him any confidence in his right to go. The urge to throw her arms around him, to make all the uncertainty go away, was strong. But Mike didn't want that. He'd made that clear enough the night before as Penny had unrolled her sleeping bag on the floor. His insistence that she take the bed was more than emphatic.

"That's not necessary," Penny had said. "That's why I brought the sleeping bag, so you could have your bed for a change."

"I'm not taking the bed while a woman sleeps on the floor," he'd insisted.

She'd chuckled. "My being a woman makes the difference, does it?"

"Don't argue with me. Just take the bed."

"Yes, Sir," she'd said, giving him a playful salute in keeping with his commanding tone, then doing as ordered.

Mike, however, had not found it amusing. From the time he'd returned from springing his traps so that no animals would be caught without anyone being around to use the meat, he had been quiet. When she'd asked him what she could do to help him prepare to leave, he gave her a couple small tasks to do, but basically he'd done everything himself with only a bare effort at congeniality in the face of her attempts at conversation.

Knowing it must be anticipation of what lay ahead that weighed on his mind, Penny had excused him. But despite his efforts to avoid the subject earlier, as they'd lain there in the darkness, she'd brought it up directly.

"Are you nervous about going back?" she'd asked.

His answer was slow in coming. "I'm fine."

"Oh, I know that," she'd said. "It's just that, well, if it was me, I would be a nervous wreck. Being away so long…things are bound to have changed while you were away. And under the circumstances, well, I would be wondering how all my friends were going to react. I mean, they probably feel pretty bad for doubting you, wondering if you'll forgive them. And you're probably–"

"Don't start analyzing me," he'd interrupted. But she ignored the firmness of his tone.

"I just want to help," she'd said. "If there is anything I can do–"

"There is."

She waited to hear it. She was willing to do anything, anything at all that he should ask her to do. But it seemed ages before he went on.

"Penny," he'd said finally, as if choosing his words carefully. "I saved your life. I know you're grateful for that and you want to repay me. But the debt is paid. You've given me back my life. We're even. So I wish you would just stop."

"Mike–"

She'd wanted to assure him that repayment was not her motive, that she was in love with him, that she only wanted to help him the way any woman would want to help the man she loved. But caution prevented her from revealing too much of her innermost feelings until she was certain how he would receive them. She couldn't risk pushing him further away.

"I mean it, Penny," he'd said when she'd grown silent. "I'm a big boy now. I can take care of myself. I don't want you waiting on me. I don't want you analyzing me. I don't want you making things easier for me. I want you to just let me go home where I belong without trying to hold my hand."

"You're…not going to take the job my father offered you, then?" she'd asked.

"No, I'm not," he'd said. "I know you went to a lot of trouble to convince your father to give me that option, and I appreciate it. But I've been away from home a long time. It's time I went back, faced my life. And I'll be fine, so you can quit worrying about me. I've been taking care of myself for a long time. I'm perfectly able to do so now as well, okay?"

"Okay," she'd said with a sigh. She had no choice. If that was the way he wanted it she had no right to argue.

"I'm glad you care, Penny," he'd said at length. "But I don't like being fussed over."

"I guess I have been a bit pushy," she'd admitted reluctantly.

"Not pushy," he'd denied kindly. "I know you've only been trying to help. But I don't need mothered, okay? It's time I took charge of my own life."

"Okay," she'd agreed.

"Goodnight, then," he'd said, and she hadn't dared to make any further attempts at conversation.

Now, as they climbed the hill, she knew her father had been right. The things Mike had been through these past two years had made it difficult, maybe impossible for him to get emotionally close to anyone again. And because he was returning almost immediately to California she would not be given time enough to ease him into such trust again.

Roy had been waiting for them in the van. But as Mike and Penny crested the top of the hill he climbed out to open the horse trailer for

Star. The two men eyed one another in the moment it took them to draw near, and as they did so Penny spoke to ease the tension between them.

"Daddy, this is Mike Klotski. Mike, my father, Roy Loftin."

Roy held out his hand with a smiled greeting. "Nice to meet you, Mike," he said with a serious air that denied his smile as Mike took his hand politely, but nervously. "I'd like to thank you for saving my daughter's life."

"She's more than repaid me, Sir," Mike said, the husky note in his voice telling Penny just how nervous he was.

As he turned to assist her from the saddle she tried to give him a boast of confidence with her smile, but he did not meet her eyes. From his next words she felt certain he was concerned about just what sort of repayment her father might suspect he had exacted from her.

"Without her I would still be running, hiding, not knowing I could safely return home. She's given me back my life as clearly as I gave her hers."

Proudly Penny watched her father react to that. The smile he turned on his daughter was relaxed as his arm wrapped around her in a fatherly hug.

"All the same, I am grateful to you for my little girl's life. If there is ever anything I can do to repay you, you have only to ask."

Turning to Star he began to remove the saddle and all that she carried on her back, including Mike's meager possessions. Everything Mike had found in the cabin he had left there. So the only things he carried back with him on his departure were the few things he had brought with him and the things Penny had made for him – her wood carvings and her straw hat.

Penny, however, had taken one item from the cabin – the old, rusty dipper containing the violets Mike had given her. "We can't leave them to die," was her excuse, but she knew the real reason was a sentimental one – because Mike had given them to her, and when he was gone from her life forever she wanted something to keep him near.

Mike assisted Roy in putting everything in the back of the van, then Roy led Star to the trailer.

"Did Penny mention that we're looking for an assistant manager at our Rogers' office?" he asked as he closed up the trailer.

"She mentioned it," Mike acknowledged. "And thank you for the offer, but it's time I went home."

Roy stared at him thoughtfully, then at his daughter, as they all piled into the van – Penny in front with her father, Mike in the seat behind. He knew Penny regretted Mike's refusal to stay, and he wished there was some way he could make her happy.

"If you think I made this offer to repay you for Penny's life, you should know that's not the case," he said as he started the engine and drove out onto the dirt road. "I built this company myself, starting when I was only seventeen. It's as important to me as any of my children, and I do not treat it lightly. When I hire someone to work for me I chose someone who will be an asset. Your club's success shows me you have the business sense I'm looking for. The fact that you saved Penny's life and took care of her at personal risk to yourself shows me you're a man to be trusted, to be relied on. Those are qualities you can't always depend on when you bring in someone new. I would be honored if you would change your mind."

Penny held her breath, hoping he would. But Mike was not swayed by her father's little speech.

"Thank you, Sir," he said from the back seat. "But I do need to be getting back. I've left my affairs too long in the hands of others as it is."

"Understandable," Roy conceded. "But I had to ask. And call me Roy. So tell me, Mike, how do you like running a fitness club? You must meet some interesting people."

For the next hour, as they made their way to Rogers, Roy kept Mike talking, mostly about business in general and his club in particular. Occasionally Penny made a comment or two when it was expected of her, but for the most part she let the men talk as a strange emptiness grew bigger and bigger inside her until she felt completely hollow.

"Mike's going back to California," the whining of the tires on the pavement droned. "You're never going to see him again. You're never going to see him again."

It was not yet five-thirty when Roy, Penny and Mike reached the Golden Sun Restaurant in Tulsa where Mike was to meet Joe at six. Mike and Penny had spent two hours eating lunch and letting him shop for new clothes and other items he needed for his trip, as well as getting his first hair cut in a year and his first proper shave. During those two hours they had talked on dozens of topics almost non-stop, as if neither of them could endure the silence, alone with their thoughts. And yet not once had either of them said what was really on their minds – Mike's reunion with his brother and his subsequent departure from her life forever.

Now, as that meeting was so eminent, Penny was glad that her father had offered to drive them on to Tulsa. The ride home would have been intolerable.

"Sam and Bea live upstairs," Roy informed Mike as they knocked on the back door of the restaurant building rather than going in through the front. "We thought you and Joe might prefer a bit of privacy for your reunion, so they've offered you the use of their apartment."

The door was opened by a rotund little woman Roy's age even as he finished speaking.

"Roy, Penny," she said with genuine delight as she greeted them each with a big hug. "It is so good to see you. And this must be Mike," she added, giving him her hand. "I'm Bea. Come in, come in."

The three of them followed her into a small carpeted hall with a door at one end and a set of stairs at the other. From previous visits Penny knew that the door led into the kitchen of the restaurant itself, but Bea now led the way up the stairs to the very nice apartment above which she shared with her husband.

"Make yourselves at home," Bea said as they reached the top of the stairs. "There's coffee in the kitchen. And we'll send up your dinner as soon as your brother arrives. In the mean time, I'd better be getting myself back to work before Sam comes looking for my hide."

Sam, as Penny knew, would never 'have her hide.' The two of them had been married for thirty-seven years and, so far as Penny knew, there had never been an impatient word between them. But her smile as she left them confirmed her lack of fear in that regard. She was only trying to leave them alone to their own business.

"I'll join you," Roy said as he followed her from the room, adding to Penny, "I'll buzz you as soon as he gets here."

"Thanks, Dad," she said, giving him a hug.

For a moment she stood watching him follow Bea to the stairs, but as the door closed behind them she turned to give Mike a smile.

"Would you care for a cup of coffee?" she asked.

"No, thanks."

As she pondered his refusal his eyes were touched by a sheepish grin. "I think I'm on a coffee high as it is from the two cups I had with lunch and I'm not sure how many yesterday and this morning. After a year without caffeine I think my body is out of practice."

"I suppose a caffeine high is unnecessary when you've got anticipation to keep your heart pumping," she smiled. "Joe isn't supposed to be here until six, so we've got about half an hour to wait. Is there anything I could get you until then?"

"No, thanks, I'm fine," he said as he paced across to the window that looked out over the street.

Not wanting to contradict him, Penny said nothing. But after just a brief pause he turned back, a half smile on his face.

"Okay, I'm not fine," he admitted. "I don't know why I'm so nervous. He's just my brother."

"And he's really looking forward to seeing you," she reminded him. "He wouldn't be coming all this way if he wasn't."

Mike gave her another smile. "And I should just relax," he said in a faraway tone, as if trying to convince himself. "So why can't I?"

"Maybe because of what Joe represents," she suggested.

Mike's eyebrow raised crookedly. Oh, how she was going to miss that look. But she dismissed the pain that went with that thought. He was silent, so she continued.

"Joe is your biggest link to the past right now," she said. "To everything that went wrong with your life before you left. But once you get past this meeting the rest will be a snap."

"You think so?" he asked, but his skeptical laugh indicated disbelief.

"I think so," she insisted, though in reality she wasn't any more sure than he was. But reassuring him seemed paramount, building his confidence. That was the key to his relaxing.

Mike, however, continued to look doubtful as he turned back to stare out through the window at the parking lot below.

"Mike, it's going to be fine," she repeated.

She was pushing again. She knew she was. And she knew it was not what he wanted from her. But she couldn't seem to help herself. This was the man she loved with all her heart. His concerns were her concerns. But he said nothing.

"Mike, what is it?" she insisted against her better judgment.

"Nothing," he said.

But she continued to push. "Mike…?"

"I'm just a coward," he said, his back to her, his tone low and self-condemning.

"Why?"

"Penny…"

He didn't turn, though his sigh of frustration was clearly audible.

"Why?" she repeated. "Because you're feeling a little nervous…?"

Turning at last to face her, his expression grew decidedly more set. "Penny, I am a coward. Not just now in facing Joe, but for the past year. I ran away. I was faced with a situation that terrified me, so I ran at the first opportunity. And I kept running until that threat was eliminated."

"Mike, that's not true…"

"Isn't it?" he asked with pained skepticism. "I not only ran, I hid from the whole world in the deepest hole I could find. And how can I face Joe's thinking I'm a coward?"

"That's crazy," Penny insisted. "Joe doesn't think of you as a coward any more than I do."

"Then what do you call it?" he asked with self-criticism. "What do you call a man who runs from his problems rather than staying to face them, a man who hides from the world rather than fighting for what's rightly his."

"Mike, you did face your problems," she denied with determination. "You fought for your rights in a court of law just like any good citizen. But the courts failed you. You were faced with a long prison term you didn't deserve, one you were prepared to endure if you had to–"

She paused as he moved slowly to sit on the sofa, but as he opened his mouth to object, she insisted, "Mike, I know you. You need to be free. You need open spaces. It would have killed you to be locked away like that, especially knowing you were innocent. You only did what you had to do."

Without looking at her he scoffed. "What I had to do."

"Does a drowning man reject a life-preserver when it's thrown to him?" she demanded. "Is it cowardice for him to accept something that's going to save his life? Or would he have to go ahead and drown to be considered brave?"

Restlessly Mike got back to his feet and paced across the room. "I wasn't dying."

"No, you were facing a fate worse than death," she said. "You were facing a life behind bars that would have driven you crazy, a life you did not deserve. You would have been a fool to ignore the door to freedom when it was dropped into your lap. And you're no fool."

For a long moment Mike just stood there staring blindly through the window while she waited for his response. His sudden chuckle sounded relieved. It certainly relieved her to see the tension relax from his shoulders.

"You're something else," he said, though he didn't turn to look at her. "I don't know why, but…"

A loud buzz interrupted him, and he turned toward the sound as Penny quickly went to the intercom by the door.

"Yes?" she said into it as she held down the button.

"He's here," Roy's voice filled the room. "There's a woman with him, but otherwise he's alone."

"Karen," Mike said quietly from his place across the room.

"Thanks, Dad," she said. "I'll be right down."

Turning to Mike she gave him a smile. "Are you ready?"

He took a deep breath. "Ready," he said.

"Then I'll bring him right up," she promised, pleased that he seemed a little less stressed then he had, though she knew he would never relax completely until this meeting was over.

"Penny?"

His voice stopped her as she opened the door. She turned back to face him.

"Thank you," he said. "For everything."

Her only response was a smile. Then she went through the door, down the stairs, and into the restaurant through the kitchen. With her heart pounding she returned her father's smile as she passed him and Sam at the grill, then stepped into the dining room.

Joe and his female companion, presumably his wife, Karen, were seated where they could watch the door, so they didn't see her until she was only a few feet from their table. It was the woman who saw her first and, though she had never seen Penny before, she seemed to know instinctively, probably from the look on Penny's face, that this was the woman for whom they were waiting. An almost indistinct movement on her part caught Joe's attention, drawing him instinctively to his feet to face this woman who was at the moment his only link to his brother.

"Is Mike with you?" he asked. His eagerness was intense.

"He's waiting for you," she said. "Is this your wife?"

"Oh, yes, Karen," he said, having completely forgotten her existence in that moment.

"It's nice to meet you," Penny said, giving Karen a smile. "If you would both like to follow me I will take you to Mike."

Quickly Karen retrieved her purse from the seat beside her, the only item either of them carried, and both followed her back between the other diners and through the kitchen.

"Is he okay?" Joe asked.

"He's fine," Penny assured him. "Anxious to see you. We just thought it might be nice for both of you if you had some privacy for your reunion."

She didn't even see her father watching her as she led Joe and Karen through the kitchen and up the back stairs. She was feeling as apprehensive as any of the others, and she could think of nothing but the hope that this meeting went as well for Mike as he wanted it to.

At the top of the stairs she opened the door, then stood back to let Joe and Karen pass inside. The apprehension Mike was feeling as he watched them enter the room was mirrored in Joe's face as he stopped and their eyes met. Penny could only stand there holding her breath as she watched the two men, both uncertain of the other's feelings. Was Mike hurt by Joe's doubting him in the past? Did Joe see Mike as a coward for running from his problems when the opportunity presented itself?

Mike was the first to break the silence. "Joe, Karen, thank you for coming all this way."

Joe cut the distance between them by a couple of steps. "Are you okay?" he asked. Mike only had a chance to nod before he added, "I was so worried when I didn't hear from you. I thought…I thought maybe you were dead."

"I'm sorry, Joe," Mike said. Penny could hear the regret in his tone. "I'm sorry for putting you through that. I know I shouldn't have run. I was a coward…"

"Of course you ran," Joe said. "You'd have been an idiot not to with only a future in prison to look forward to. You deserved better than that. You deserved… Mike, I am so sorry for doubting you. I should have known. I should have believed in you."

Mike gave him a smile – nervous, but a smile nevertheless. "It did look pretty bad."

"Still, I should have believed in you," Joe insisted. "You're my brother, my only family. I should have known you couldn't–"

"You did stand by me," Mike reminded him. "Even with your doubts you stood by me, my big brother. I'll always be grateful to you for that. Thank you. And thank you for coming here now."

As he spoke he held out his hand to his brother, to bridge the gap of misunderstanding and mistrust between them. But as Joe took his hand, suddenly they found themselves embracing in a warm, heartfelt, brotherly hug, and it was then that Penny decided to return downstairs. They were going to be all right. They didn't need her.

"Penny?" Mike's voice stopped her. "You're not leaving?" It

sounded like a plea, causing her heart to skip a beat. He still needed her. The smile she gave him reflected the warmth his words had created in her.

"I thought I would go down and bring up your dinner," she informed him.

"Will you join us?"

She hadn't planned to join them. This was a family occasion. Her plan had been to join her father downstairs. But if Mike needed her–

"We would like to have you join us," Joe said as she looked for his and Karen's reaction to the invitation.

"I'll be right back," she promised. Then she hurried down the stairs with a warm glow in her heart. Maybe Mike wouldn't forget her too quickly, even when he did return to California with his brother.

Several seconds of silence passed as Mike stared after Penny. She had done what she'd set out to do. She'd restored his freedom, she'd reunited him with his brother. Her debt to him was paid. Surely she no longer felt any obligation toward him for saving her life. When he returned to the home he had left so long ago she would forget him.

"Your friend seems very nice," Karen commented, speaking for the first time.

"Penny," he said, savoring the sound of her name as he forced his attentions back to Joe and his wife. "Yes, she's great."

"Is there anything…?" Joe started, then hesitated over the words.

But Mike knew what was on his mind. "There's nothing," he said with regret. "I saved her life. She's grateful. That's all. So, how are the kids?"

Both Joe and Karen looked as if they would like to pursue the subject of Penny, but it was clear that Mike did not. So, to his relief, they left it alone, turning to the subject to which he had changed it.

"They're fine," Karen said in answer to his question. "All three of them."

"Three?" Mike asked in surprise. He knew about Peter and Annie. But a third?

"Michaella," Joe said. "She was seven weeks old yesterday."

As that unexpected news hit him, Mike dropped to the nearest seat, a forest green ottoman.

"I have been away a long time, haven't I?" he said. It had seemed an eternity while he was out there all alone. And yet the knowledge that another life had been conceived and born in that time seemed to make it that much longer.

"We named her after her Uncle Michael," Karen said. "In the hope that you might forgive us for not believing in you."

Mike looked up at her, then at Joe. The fact that his new niece's name was a form of his own hadn't even registered on his mind.

"I'm honored," he said with sincerity. "But honestly, you don't have to keep apologizing—"

Joe came to sit on the nearby sofa, Karen taking her place beside him. "Mike, I do owe you an apology," he insisted. "You told me you were innocent. I should have believed you from the very beginning. I should never have let the circumstantial evidence cause me to doubt my own brother."

"It was pretty damning," Mike said. "I understand your doubts. I don't blame you. I was just grateful to you for standing by me. I don't think I could have made it through everything if you hadn't been there for me."

Joe seemed to feel the gratitude undeserved, but he didn't insist. Instead he said, "I was worried about you. Being in jail that short time you were before bail was set had already had an affect on you – that and everything else you were going through. I was afraid prison – being confined to a cell, day after day – I was afraid it would drive you over the edge."

Mike got to his feet to pace to the window. "I thought so, too," he said quietly. "I suppose that's the real reason I took the coward's way out and ran at the first opportunity."

"That wasn't an act of cowardice, Michael," Karen said.

Mike turned and would have denied it, but Joe gave him no opportunity to do so. "She's right, Mike. It might have been cowardice if you'd run after being released on bail – before giving the courts a chance, but you didn't do that. Despite the fact that all the evidence was against you and not a soul believed in you, you stayed. You faced the consequences with dignity. You faced a jury even when you had very little hope of being believed. I don't know if I could have done that."

"But when that failed I ran," he reminded him.

"You only took what was rightfully yours," Karen said. "Freedom."

"Prison would have killed you," Joe added. "You could never sit in your office for more than an hour before the need for freedom would send you outside. It wasn't cowardice. It was self-preservation. No one blames you, you had to go."

Mike turned back to the window. "So Penny said."

"She's obviously a smart woman who knows you well," Joe said behind him.

"You're fortunate she loves you so much," Karen observed.

"She's not in love with me," Mike said quietly, a deep ache in his heart that prevented him from facing them. "I saved her life. She's grateful. She felt she owed me. That's all."

"Did she tell you that?" Karen asked.

"She didn't have to," Mike insisted, growing uncomfortable with the change the conversation had taken. "I know."

"Don't be too sure, Mike," Joe said. "She went to an awful lot of trouble to help you–"

"I saw the look in her eyes," Karen said. "No woman ever looked at a man that way unless she was in love with him."

"Talk to her, Mike," Joe said. "Tell her how you feel."

Mike's eyes turned to those of his brother, begging to believe his words. If only it was possible that Penny might really care about him his whole world would finally be perfect.

"Don't let her go out of your life without at least telling her how you feel," Karen said. "At least give her a chance."

The sound of footsteps on the stairs cut off her words, but they were enough to start Mike thinking. Was it possible? Did Penny really have personal feelings for him? If not, confessing his own feelings would only serve to embarrass them both. But was there a chance? Did he dare risk it?

The door opened, and there she was, followed by a waiter, each of them carrying trays of food which they placed on the table in the dining area of the room.

"It certainly smells good," Joe commented.

Penny acknowledged his words with a smile, then turned to thank the waiter who took both trays and departed.

"Aren't you joining us after all?" Karen asked Penny. It was only then that Mike realized she had only provided dinner for three. His heart sank.

"I'm sorry," she said. "My father just got a call. He has to get back to attend to some business. But feel free to make yourselves at home. When you've finished just buzz Sam on the intercom here and he'll send someone up for the dishes. They close the restaurant downstairs at eleven. But feel free to use the apartment until then."

"Thank you," Joe said, his tone echoing the formal air she had suddenly taken on.

"It's too bad you can't stay," Karen said. "I was looking forward to our getting to know each other."

Joe echoed her sentiment. "We have so much to thank you for."

"There's no need to thank me for anything," she denied. "I only did what I had to do."

Turning to Mike she added, "Goodbye, Mike. Have a safe trip home. And if you're not too busy maybe you could give me a call sometime. I'd like to hear how everything turns out. You can get my number from Sam and Bea, or from information."

For a moment she stared at him, but the fact that she was leaving him filled him with such a strong, empty longing that he could do nothing but stare back at her. She turned to Joe and Karen.

"It was nice meeting you," she said. "Have a good trip home."

And then she was gone, her footsteps on the stairs echoing the loneliness in his heart.

"Go after her," Joe said in a low tone. "Talk to her."

Mike only stared at the closed door until he could hear her footsteps no longer. Suddenly he knew he could not let it end there. Penny not only had given him back his life, she was his life. Without conscious thought or consideration for Joe and Karen, he found himself bounding down the stairs after her. As he opened the outer door and stepped out into the sunshine, she was just getting into the car where her father was already waiting.

"Penny!"

He knew he must sound like mad man hollering at her that way, but there was no hint in her face that she thought his behavior anything but normal as she turned to face him.

Now what? "I...I didn't...I wanted to say goodbye," he stuttered like a fool. "And to thank you...for everything."

"I'm glad I could help," she said seriously, though she smiled.

"I just..."

If only he could think what to say to her. If only her father wasn't right there, in a hurry, listening to every inane word he uttered.

"I will call you," he promised.

"I would like that."

She seemed sincere enough in saying that, her eyes never leaving his. Some incredibly powerful force seemed to be drawing him even closer to her, or her to him, he wasn't sure which. All he knew was an incredible desire to pull her close, to kiss her sweet, luscious lips, to confess to her his deepest feelings.

But her father was there, right there, listening to every word, even while he was trying to be inconspicuous. How could a man confess his love in the presence of the father of the very woman to whom his heart cried out? Did she even want to hear it?

"Goodbye, Mike," she said finally when he could only seem to stare at her. "I'll never forget you...that you saved my life."

She started to turn away from him, to climb into the car beside her father, and suddenly he could control himself no longer. Before thought could prevent him, he found himself pulling her into his arms, kissing her as he had wanted to do for as long as he could remember. Whether she responded or not he was unaware. He knew only that holding her felt incredibly perfect. Tasting the sweetness of her lips like tasting the wines of the Gods. She was what his whole body craved, what his soul and heart coveted.

And then reality hit as his subconscious became aware of a

movement from inside the car behind her. Her father. This was not the time or the place for such behavior.

Slowly, reluctantly, he released her to look down into her face. But the look he was there was one of shock, and suddenly he knew what a fool he had been to give in to his passions. Now, rather than remembering him fondly, she was going to hate him.

"I'm sorry," he muttered stupidly. Then he turned away from her before he could do or say anything more to further humiliate himself and embarrass her.

"Mike?"

But he didn't stop. He didn't turn back. He couldn't face the condemnation he knew he would see there.

"I'm not sorry," she called after him. But he knew it was only pity that moved her to say that, gratitude for saving her life, pity for the miserable man that he was, and he did not turn back even to watch her drive away beside her father.

Chapter Twelve

As Mike walked in through the back door of his house he felt emotionally drained. It was the end of his third week at home. His life was beginning to regain some order. He spent his days at the club as he had so long ago, and his friends and Joe were doing all they could to make it up to him for having doubted his innocence. But nothing seemed to be able to pull him out of the depression that filled him daily.

The causes of his depression were many. Every time he entered his living room the vision of Diane's lifeless body lying on the floor filled him with nausea. Every night he spent in the bed they had once shared was filled with restless dreams, leaving him tired and miserable throughout the day.

In an attempt to keep his mind on other things he tried to keep busy, spending much of his time at the club even when he knew Jack Stone was doing a superb job in caring for all the business involved. His evenings were spent with Joe and the kids, or with his friends who couldn't seem to do enough for him. But nothing was the same as it had once been and he couldn't shake the restless feelings that filled him constantly.

When he had gone to prison he had given Joe power of attorney to handle his business affairs, and Joe had done such a good job of it that everything seemed to run itself. Mike was not needed for anything, and socializing alone – without his wife at his side as she had been in the past, without even a date for company – made him feel every bit as alone as he had out there in the wilds of the forest.

But with all of that, it was missing Penny that wore him down the most. Nearly every moment he was thinking of her, wondering how she was doing, wishing he dared call her just to hear her voice, and regretting painfully that last stupid impulse that had driven him to kiss her.

Never would he forget that look of shock that had filled her face then. She had despised him for his feelings as he'd known she would, as any woman rightly would. She had been kind to a man who had been kind to her, but love was another story. He had been a fool to listen to the hopes of his heart.

As he walked into the den, where he had been spending much of his time lately, his eyes rested on the straw hat that had been her gift to him. Without conscious thought he picked it up from it's place on top the television, fondling it absentmindedly.

It was far from fashionable. The uneven shape was only accentuated by the poor quality of the straw. It didn't even fit him particularly well. And yet it was the greatest gift he had ever received in his life because it had come from Penny.

The sound of the doorbell echoed through the house, but he ignored it as he sat in his chair in front of the blank television with the hat in his hands. He was in no mood for visitors just now, wanting only to be alone with his thoughts of Penny.

Penny. She was the greatest thing that had ever come into his life. At times it was her gentle, kind nature that made him unable to forget her. At times it was her bullying and teasing him that filled his mind and heart – as on the day of the rain storm when they had played cards nearly all day, or after she had learned his secret and had refused to leave him because he had needed her.

But he needed her now, as well. Everything about her had filled him with love for her, love as he had never known before. And yet she did not return his feelings, and he knew it was with reason. He was unworthy of her love. As Diane had so rightly pointed out, he was unworthy of being loved by any woman, least of all one as wonderful as Penny.

And yet he had dared to touch her. Knowing she would despise him for doing so he had, nonetheless, dared to kiss her as they had parted. And that one foolish act had doomed him forever to be haunted by the look on her face. If only he had not–

"Mike?"

Startled, he looked up from the hat in his hands to find Joe standing in the open doorway.

"You didn't answer the bell," Joe said, concern, not accusation, in his tone.

Mike shrugged. "I wasn't in the mood for company."

But Joe refused to take the hint, coming instead to sit in the chair next to his brother.

"Why don't you give her a call?" he suggested, well aware that Mike's thoughts were on Penny as he fondled the hat she had made for him.

Mike made no pretense of misunderstanding what he meant. "She doesn't want to hear from me."

"She said she did," Joe reminded him.

With a miserable laugh Mike put the hat away from him on the lamp table beside his chair and, as if he couldn't sit there with his thoughts any more, he got to his feet to pace to the window.

"That was before I kissed her."

"You kissed her?"

Joe hadn't been aware of that. He had been aware as Mike had returned to the apartment above the restaurant after saying goodbye to her that he was feeling lost and empty without her, but he had not known about the kiss.

"I kissed her," Mike repeated. "And now she despises me."

"Did she say so?"

"She didn't have to say so," Mike said impatiently. "It was written all over her face. I kissed her and she just stood there staring at me in shock and horror."

Even with his back to him, Joe was aware of the anguish he was feeling. "Are you sure?" he asked, unable to believe that of the woman he had met, the woman who had looked at Mike as if he was the only man alive. He would have sworn she adored him completely, that she would have welcomed Mike's kiss. Surely she had not been repulsed by it as Mike thought she was.

"Maybe you misunderstood."

"I didn't misunderstand," Mike insisted. "I kissed her and she just stood there staring."

As the pain of the memory stung him he stopped. He would never forget that look in her face as long as he lived. Nor would he ever stop regretting what he had done to put it there.

"Had you ever kissed her before?" Joe asked, trying to make him see reason.

"Of course not," Mike said. "If I had–"

"Had you ever even given her any indication how you feel about her?" Joe interrupted. "Any indication at all?"

"Joe…," Mike began, turning on him impatiently. But Joe refused to be stopped.

"No, I don't think you did," he continued. "Diane really did a number on you, didn't she? Her warped, twisted mind hurled accusations at you to cover her own guilt, and you believed every word she said. She's got you believing that no woman could ever love you."

"I saw the look on her face!" Mike insisted. "You didn't!"

"And did it ever occur to you that maybe she was just surprised when you kissed her because you had never given her any reason to expect it. She's only–"

"You have no idea what you're talking about," Mike said, impatiently turning back to the window.

"I think it's you who's confused," Joe insisted. "You've been hurt, and the wounds of that hurt go deep. You want Penny to love you. You need her to do so. But the more you need it, the more you want it, the more terrified you feel."

Mike would have protested, but Joe refused to let him.

"Mike, you're my brother," he said with determination. "I would give anything to take away the last two years, to keep you from being hurt so badly. But we can't any of us go back. All we can do is go forward. I know you're terrified of giving in to feelings that may not be returned. And I know that's blinding you to the truth. You're seeing what you expect to see, not what–"

As the ringing of the phone interrupted him, he looked expectantly at Mike, waiting for him to answer it.

"Mike?" he said when his brother made no move to do so.

"I have no intention of talking to anyone," Mike said. "The answering machine with get it. And you're wasting your time. Penny has no feelings for me at all. I saved her life. She was grateful, so she did what she could to repay me for that. But personally she has–"

Suddenly he stopped, his thoughts and his brother instantly forgotten as the beautiful voice of the woman in question filled the room while she left her message on his machine.

"Mike?"

Just that one word spoken in her sweet voice and he felt his whole body come alive. Yet he did not move, he couldn't move. He may even have stopped breathing, but he was unaware of it.

"It's me, Penny," she said.

There was some hesitation in her voice, as if she was unsure just what to say, or maybe she just didn't like answering machines. But she continued anyway.

"I hadn't heard from you. I suppose you have an awful lot to do after being gone so long. I hope everything is going okay. If you get a chance, maybe you could give me a call and let me know. Well, goodbye."

There was the briefest pause, as if she was about to hang up, then as an afterthought she left her telephone number.

When she finally hung up Mike stood staring at the silent phone like a fool.

"Mike, that was not a woman regretting a kiss," Joe said with quiet confidence. "That was a woman regretting not having heard from the man who gave her that kiss."

But Mike only stared at the phone, trying not to let the hope rise in his heart for fear it was untrue, yet knowing the hope was there nonetheless. Penny had called him. She had once asked him to call her, but when he had not done so for three weeks she had not waited any longer. Even after that kiss she had called him.

"Mike, she's in love with you," Joe insisted, concerned by his silence. "Diane has already robbed you of two years of your life. Don't let her rob you of your happiness for the rest of it as well. Penny is not Diane. She loves you – really loves you. I would bet my life on that. Call her, or you will be hurting her as much as you're hurting yourself."

Penny loved him. Did he dare to believe that? Without conscious awareness he picked up her hat, again caressing and fondling it as if it was a reassuring link to Penny that would give him the answers he longed for so badly.

"Call her," Joe said again, quieter now, as if he saw that hope was beginning to take hold in his brother's heart and that it only needed a little more of a boost to fill him completely.

Mike looked up at him at last.

"Call her," Joe said again.

Mike's eyes moved to the phone, but he hesitated as he looked back at his brother.

"Not with my brother standing over me, eavesdropping on every word," he said.

Joe gave him a smile, then came over to clasp him on the shoulder. "I get the message," he said. "And I'm on my way."

He gave Mike a quick, brotherly hug, then turned to leave.

"She'll be good for you," he added, turning back at the open doorway. "She'll make you happy. Maybe she'll even be able to make up to you for all the hurt the rest of us have caused you."

Then Joe was gone, and a moment later Mike heard the back door close behind him. But even as he began to dial Penny's number he changed his mind. Calling wasn't the answer. He would never know what to say. Besides, he had things to do.

As the days passed since Mike's return, he had been a source of interest to a lot of people. The employees and the patrons of the club were all curious about him, all speculating on what he had been doing for the past year, what had taken him so long to return, what had finally prompted his return more than six months after the verdict against him had been overturned. But Mike had not bothered to satisfy their curiosity.

Even to his friends he was evasive. The past two years of his life had been a nightmare he had no wish to discuss with anyone, least of all with people who wouldn't understand. Even to Joe he told only the barest facts – where he had been and that he had managed fine were nearly the extent of his story. Even his rescuing Penny – something Joe had been especially curious about since Mike had insisted that was her only reason for helping him learn that he had his freedom – had been a brief, bare facts monologue just to ease his brother's concern.

So, when a nosy reporter named Dick Rabin from the L.A. News Flash insisted on pressuring him from the beginning for an interview he had been very adamant in his refusal even to talk to the man. More than a week after Penny's call, however, Dick Rabin managed to corner him in a manner that made him impossible to avoid.

It was a Friday evening. For the past week he had been working hard at getting certain things arranged and that evening he was prepared to celebrate the progress he was making. For the first time since he'd returned he felt he had finally taken back control of his life, and he was just leaving the realty office where he'd spent the past hour – on his way to share the news with Joe – when the man accosted him in the parking lot.

"Mr. Klotski," Dick Raben said without any pretense at being friendly. "Could you tell me what has happened to Denise Spears?"

"What?"

Despite himself Mike was startled by the question. Denise Spears? He didn't even know a Denise Spears, but he was aware that this man was determined to get a story. Was he now making things up to rile Mike into a confession? Mike wasn't about to let him get away with it. But neither did he want the man starting rumors that would make him more trouble.

"You know, the woman you're supposed to be marrying," Raben said. "The woman who tried to make wedding arrangements at the Sweet Eternity Wedding Chapel nearly four weeks ago and has never been seen again. Maybe you can tell me how you happened to be going to marry this woman one minute and the next she disappears from the face of the earth."

Suddenly Mike understood. This was the reporter who had bothered Penny while she was here, when she had gone to the chapel to avoid being caught out and thus exposing him prematurely. Suddenly he found the man terribly amusing. He thought he was so smart in learning the name of the mystery woman in Mike's life, and yet he was so wrong it was funny.

Without bothering to answer the man he continued toward his car, but Raben was not so easily ignored.

"Denise Spears amuses you, does she?" he asked as he followed.

"No, not Denise, you," Mike said, not bothering to hold back his smile.

"I amuse you?" Raben asked. "In what way?"

"Only that you think you're so smart and yet you have no idea how one pretty, little woman pulled the wool right over your eyes," Mike said as he slipped the key into the lock on his car door.

"You're saying you had nothing to do with this woman at all?" Raben asked.

"Not at all," Mike said. "I'm only saying she isn't Denise Spears. She isn't Denise anyone. She just got tired of you following her so she made up a pretty story to drive you crazy. I'm glad to see it worked."

As Raben stood there looking confused and uncertain about whether Mike was telling him the truth or not, he climbed into the car, closing the door firmly between them.

"Then who is she?" Raben called through the closed window. "Are you marrying her? Why would she say such a thing? Who is she?!"

But Mike ignored him as he drove away. No, he was not marrying any 'Denise Spears.' He may never marry again. But if he did, there was only one woman he would ever even consider asking to be his wife.

"Penny, come on," Tina Stihls said with that demanding tone only the best of friends dared use with each other. "Talk to me. I'm not going away until you tell me everything."

"I've already told you everything," Penny said without enthusiasm.

"You told me about Caroline trying to kill you, leaving you for dead where Mike found you and rescued you," Tina agreed. "You told me all about Mike, how he was convicted of murdering his wife when he hadn't really done it at all. You even told me how you helped him get his freedom."

"All I did was tell him that the conviction had been reversed," Penny said.

But Tina continued as if she hadn't spoken. "You didn't tell me you were in love with the man, but that I could figure out for myself so I forgive you. All I want to know is what you intend doing about it. It's been a month now since you sent the guy home. So when are you going to call him?"

"I did."

Tina's eyes widened in surprise. "You did? You called him? Why didn't you tell me? What did he say? Was he glad to hear from you?"

Restlessly Penny got to her feet, pacing to the window. Her apartment seemed increasingly confining lately, especially in the face of her friend's prying.

"Penny?"

As Tina grew concerned in the silence, Penny turned to face her.

"He didn't say anything," she said. "He wasn't home. I just left a message on his machine."

"What kind of message?" Tina asked.

In the same restless spirit she had been unable to shake in all these weeks, Penny again took a seat on the sofa, just staring at her hands as the empty feelings filled her.

"I said, 'Hi, I just called to see how things were going,' and maybe he could give me a call if he wasn't too busy."

"And you haven't heard from him?"

Again Penny's restlessness brought her to her feet to pace across the floor, this time to the corner of the room that served as her kitchen where she poured herself another cup of tea.

"I haven't heard from him," she admitted. "I'm not going to hear from him. He's back in his own world now where he belongs. Me, the whole…thing in the woods, we're just a crazy memory to be put behind him. There's no reason at all–"

"Penny." Tina got to her feet to join her, refilling her own cup as well. "Maybe he just needs…"

The ringing of the doorbell cut her off and Penny, glad for the interruption to this depressing conversation, turned to answer it. Habitually she looked through the peep hole before opening the door, but as she did so now she stopped in surprise, shock at the sight of her visitor.

Immediately Tina, aware of the change in her, was at her side. "Who is it?" she asked in whispered excitement. "Is it him?"

Penny didn't have to answer. It was clear in her eyes, in the flushed excitement of her face, in the sudden pounding of her heart.

"So let him in," Tina whispered.

But Penny couldn't seem to move. Why was he here? He hadn't written. He hadn't called. Not in more than four weeks. He hadn't even returned the call she'd made to him. Now suddenly he was standing on her doorstep? She needed a minute to clear her head before facing him, to compose herself enough that she would be able to keep from throwing herself into his arms the minute the door was opened, before she was even certain why he was here.

But Tina wasn't waiting. As the knock sounded again she reached for the knob herself, opening the door to meet this man who was having such a strong effect in her friend.

"You must be Mike," she said to the man in front of her.

When Penny had first seen him through the peephole he was been wearing her straw hat, but now, clearly surprised to find the woman greeting him was not the one he had been expecting, though Penny was standing a bit behind the open door, embarrassment made him remove it.

"I'm Tina. Please, come in. I was just leaving."

Her abrupt departure was so obvious as to be embarrassing to Penny, but there was nothing she could do about it now, and she was unable to read Mike's face to determine how he felt about this clear attempt to encourage a relationship between her and this male visitor of hers.

"Hello," Penny said, nervously finding her voice as Tina hurried away. "Would you like to come in?"

Of course he would, she chided herself as he thanked her and stepped inside. He hadn't come all this way to stand in the hall.

"Can I get you anything?" she asked. "Coffee? Tea? Cola?"

"Whatever you're having," he said agreeably with a nod toward the two cups of tea she and Tina had just poured.

The fact that they were still full made Tina's sudden departure that much more suspicious. The least she could have done was to finish her tea, but to comment on the obvious was to make the situation even more embarrassing, so instead she tried to appear calmer than she felt.

"It's an oriental Herbal tea," she told him.

"Sounds good."

There was no enthusiasm for the tea in his tone, but she had a feeling it was more a distraction with regard to the purpose of his visit then an actual dislike of her offered refreshment.

"Please, have a seat," she offered as she moved toward the kitchenette to pour his tea, but rather than taking her up on her invitation, he followed her.

"I got your message," he said behind her. "I'm sorry I didn't return your call sooner."

Nervously she poured his tea, concentrating on controlling the shaky impulses that filled her so as not to spill it.

"I didn't expect you to answer in person," she said, smiling, trying to sound casual as she turned to hand him the cup of tea.

Their eyes met, and in that instant the smile dropped from her face as a strong anticipation came over her, hope filling her heart as his eyes searched deep into her soul.

"I couldn't say what I wanted to say over the phone," he said as he took the cup from her. The unusually deep tone of his voice combined with the strong emotion mirrored in his eyes had the effect of mesmerizing her, rooting her to the spot.

"So much has happened these past weeks," he said somewhere in the eons that followed as they seemed locked in each other's eyes. "Business to take care of, people to see, a house to sell."

"You…sold your house?" Her eyes grew wide. What was he saying?

"I sold my house," he repeated, his eyes never leaving her face. "I bought a new one–a ranch about thirty miles outside of the city. Lots of wide open spaces, room for some horses and gardening, walking… A place to build new memories."

"Oh."

It was only natural after his ordeal that the house he had shared with Diane would seem confining and full of bad memories. But somehow she had hoped his plans had involved her.

"A place to start over," he said. "To build a new life, with…with a new wife…?"

As his eyes held hers his words faded away, but they echoed on in her brain. A new wife? What was he saying to her? What new wife? Did she dare to believe…?

Slowly, as she stood glued to the spot in some sort of trance, he reached over to place his untouched cup of tea on the counter, never taking his eyes from her face. Penny didn't move, she wasn't even certain she was breathing as his gentle finger reached up to caress her cheek. The fact that she didn't flinch away from him seemed to give him courage.

"I do love you, Penny," he said, his tone so deeply emotional it was as if he spoke directly to her heart, bypassing her ears completely. "I tried not to. I had nothing to offer you. I…You gave me back my life. But it means nothing to me if you're not there to share it with me. I…Maybe I'm rushing you. I know you haven't known me long, and I'll wait–"

Suddenly she could stand it no longer. Mike loved her. He wanted her in his life. There was nothing in the world of greater importance than that. She threw herself in his arms and, though surprised by her impulsive action, he put his arms around her, drawing her close as she wanted to be.

"Oh, Mike," she breathed. "I thought I would never see you again. And I love you so much–"

He just held her, hardly daring to believe the extent of her feelings or that of his own good fortune. Penny loved him. She really loved him. And now he had something to offer her. She was his, and their future together had just begun.

Printed in the United Kingdom
by Lightning Source UK Ltd.
122309UK00001B/66/A